11.5.11

To Queen Mom
please excuse
the editing mista
The publisher says the
award is still out there
is perfect novel.
have done better.
the read.
for the
They should
I hope you enjoy
Tom's friend
Patrick

Louisburg Sluggers

Louisburg Sluggers

A Novel

Bill Vanderbeck
Patrick J. Joyce

A Product of E Gate Productions
1051 Beacon Street   Suite 204
Brookline, Massachusetts 02146

Registered with The Library of Congress

ISBN- 0983372411
ISBN-13- 9780983372417

Electronic book available at http://www.amazon.com/

Manufactured in the United States of America

Heartfelt Thanks to

David Replogle, Rosanne Joyce, Lenny Gillis and Steve Gordon
who always believed in the novel.

A special thanks to Lyle Montague whose assistance with
both the electronic and print versions was invaluable.

Patricia Downey Mack, Editor
Nancy Berry, Copy Editor
Chris Faust, Cover Artist
Elizabeth Abitbol, Design Coordinator

Take me out to the ball game.
Take me out with the crowd.
Buy me some peanuts and Cracker Jack.
I don't care if I ever get back.
Let me root, root, root for the home team,
If they don't win it's a shame.
For it's one, two, three strikes, you're out
At the old ball game.

Jack Norworth
(1908)

Narrator's
Introduction

I love Baseball. Most Americans love Baseball. It's more American than any sport. It demands everything from the individual for the sake of the team. Size, power, speed, intelligence, they're always in play, but during any play one of those elements can negate the others. Like this great country, Baseball is not bound by constraints. Not even time. Teams play until one wins regardless of how long it takes.

When I was a kid I'd go to sleep thinking about Baseball and wake up thinking about it. It seemed Baseball was always alive. And like anything living, it changes. Fans revel in the change. They argue about the rules. They bicker about the players. They compare the present to the past as they look to the future.

Like any institution, it has its ups and downs, times that elevate the players and fans to a level that transcends the tedium of everyday life and allow, if only for a brief moment, the feeling that all of us are better than we really are. But like most human activities, Baseball has its dark side as well, and places the shame of not being on the up and up in our faces like nothing else can. Players expect more from Baseball. Fans expect more from Baseball. Let's face it, Americans expect more from Baseball. After all, it's *Our National Game.*

Now that we're in the twenty-first century with its ever growing number of high tech devices and rapid change, Baseball has taken on even a more important role. In trying to keep up with the innovations that creep into every aspect of contemporary life, the fans look to those special moments dispersed throughout each year from early April through late October. They step into the parks and out of their tedium to separate themselves from the manic movement, and for a brief period find solace in the suspension of time. In those moments the twenty-first century could be the twentieth, or even the nineteenth century, when all eyes view the field forgetting the rest of their surroundings, and focus on a mound sixty-feet-six inches from a white pentangle, as they wait for the stillness of a carefully planned scheme to break into a fluid, spontaneous movement.

Only then do the players disregard their bids for astronomical salaries. Only then do the owners dismiss their investments and like the rest of the crowd move to the edge of their seats in nervous anticipation. Only then do the fans stand and scream with total abandon, or sit breathlessly and quietly contain the pride and emotion they hold for their team. Only then are all of them magically captivated by *The Game*.

The best example of that magic I ever saw happened a few years back in my hometown of Boston. At that time, Fenway Park hadn't changed much since it was so well built back in 1912. Even as a young adult when I took my usual seat in the right field bleachers or was lucky enough to sit in one of the boxes where I could almost touch the players, I still got the same nostalgic thrill I had when I was a kid. That year the Sox were playing out the season the same as usual until the Fourth of July when a bunch of local boys had a sweeping effect on them and the rest of the town as well. In fact, they had an effect on everyone they came in contact with that summer. I always hear in my mind's ear the strains of John Kiley's organ playing that old chestnut, *Take*

Me Out To The Ballgame, when I think about those boys, and even though they're grown men now with children of their own, I can still see and hear their playful banter back when...

Boston is a Sports Town – but for many – Baseball is the only game in Town.

The sounds of games being played and blossoming of magnolias – but winter-weary Bostonians – that Spring is here.

~1~

A robin's song softly settled onto the quiet narrow streets of Boston's Beacon Hill as a black limousine cruised by the blossoming magnolias over the cobblestone streets of Louisburg Square, the most prestigious address in the most revered section of the city. As soon as it reached a full stop, three passenger doors flew open and a teenage boy emerged from each.

Aside from being dressed the same in their Buckingham, Brown and Nichols uniforms, marking them as private school boys, three more unlikely looking comrades could not consciously be chosen. Blond Roger Gray with his clean cut preppie look and attitude seemed like he was being groomed to assume leadership. Cecil Underwood, also clean cut and an intellect far beyond his years, sported the blue blazer, chinos and school tie with equal ease defying all stereotypes of an African American teen. Harmon Hudson was definitely a computer the geek of the group. He couldn't even get out of the car without dropping his school bag and tripping over his own feet.

But Harmon knew computers.

As they ran for their respective front doors, Roger turned and yelled, "Corner in fifteen minutes.

A laughing Cecil seized the opportunity to playfully tease his clumsy friend. "Hustle up, Harmon. We don't have all day."

Harmon hiked up his belt over his thin frame, picked up his bag, pushed back his glasses and sheepishly smiled at the chauffer. ¶The boys weren't accustomed to such service, but the school's administration had offered Harmon's father, a respected professor at the renowned M.I.T. Intelligence Lab, the perk in exchange for his making a presentation on the latest strides in Artificial Intelligence. He in turn instructed the driver to take the boys home after dropping him at his office.

As we all know, looks, and especially first impressions, can be extremely deceiving. The boys' common connections more than overrode their differences. Most importantly, all three were good guys, the kind who could be depended on over the

These boys had more things in common

6

long haul. Next, even though none of them could play very well, they loved baseball. Even more, they loved girls, especially Roger who found it difficult to concentrate on anything else when a pretty young lady was near.

But for now, they were only interested in one thing. Baseball.

At the same time on the other side of town, Jo Lugo yelled at one of her ballplayers from the top of the front stairwell of South End High School.

"Luther."

The shrewd fifteen-year old determinedly sped down the stairs. This prompted and even louder, "Luther Gordon."

A frustrated, delayed Luther could tell by the tone that he had better stop and respond. Hearing his full name he knew Miss Lugo meant business and like the other boys in the school he was captivated by the beautiful woman in her early thirties who not only could teach but was, of all things, the boys' baseball coach. She was not one to be taken lightly.

"Yes, Miss Lugo."

"Did you finish your math?"

"Done."

"English?"

"Done."

"Biology?"

Luther was becoming progressively more frustrated to the point he was sorry he'd stopped. "It's all done, Miss Lugo," he said dropping his shoulders, stooping over and walking slowly with his arms dangling by his sides. "Honest."

"You gotta make grades if you want to play ball."

Realizing his break, Luther straightened up, turned and sped down the four steps to the door while yelling back, "I will. I will. Don't worry."

The outside air had never felt better to Luther as he escaped through the door and raced across the concrete entry of the three story brick building that for the past few hours had been his academic prison. As soon as he hit the bottom of the side steps, he ran even faster across the asphalt parking lot and under the overpass that opened into the school's ballfield. He smiled as he approached his best friend Richie D'Angelo who everyone called D.A.

○K (Luther and D.A.) were physical opposites. The latter was a tall sixteen year old with a large natural athletic build and the visual acuity of a slugger. But unlike most early bloomers, he had an edge that would continue to develop for years to come. He stood near the plate with a bat in his hand patiently waiting for his friend by hitting balls into the backstop.

8

"You're late," D.A. said in a half mocking tone.

"So what? I'm here now."

"Where you been?"

"Where you should have been," he chided. "Studying."

D.A. extended his bat indifferently looking at the Louisville Slugger trademark on the grain.

"I do my studying right here on the field," he confidently stated, "but you're doing good listening to Miss Lugo. A major league ballplayer needs a good agent and a good agent needs his math."

D.A. winked at the now smiling Luther. "Me and you are going all the way to the top."

Luther reached down, picked up one of the balls and in a smooth motion leaned forward and tossed it over his back and head. "Whatta ya say, D.A.?"

With immediate focus and pure concentration, D.A. swung the bat with the controlled, fluid motion of a power hitter. As the ball rose it seemed to take on a life of its own sailing well over 300 feet hitting the back of the large metal sign tacked to a light post. The sign read WELCOME TO BOSTON.

9

Kate - 10 years old

30 years   (40)

Jo - 30 - 5

One of the many antique shop in (Beacon Hill) Charles Street

30 yrs

~2~

Yisted this wo a antique shop

at

ambience

special

distinctive

atmosphere

balling coach

Late

The late spring afternoon sun shed just enough light on the wooden sign of Yesterday's News to lend the ambiance deserved by an antiques shop located in the oldest section of the city at the foot of Beacon Hill. The shop was going into its third decade and the owner, Nate Lugo, was more surprised than anyone at the longevity seldom enjoyed by most Charles Street businesses. The surprise was unwarranted. Throughout Nate Lugo's life, success had been the norm. The thickly built seventy-year old carried an air of strength equaled only by the confident attitude of his male English bulldog, Gunner.

Antique Shoppe

Red Sox batting coach

Gunner, leash in mouth, ambled through the curtain from the back room, around the expensive antique furniture, stained glass and artwork stuffed into the up-market establishment. He dropped the

Nate Lugo real dragon

leash at Nate's feet and expectantly looked up at his owner. The old man smiled, leaned over and offered him a Fenway Frank. Well familiar with this daily ritual, Gunner gulped the frank, pleased to be fed and ready to be aired. As Gunner chewed, Nate hooked the leather strap to his collar.

"Come on, Boy. Let's go for a walk."

Freddy Dunster, Nate's business partner and closest friend, peered over his glasses and momentarily left his precise bookkeeping to watch the routine. Freddy, a blue-blood Yankee entrepreneur, was pure New England from his tweeds and bow tie down to his brogues. Business-wise, he was smart, competitive and well versed in antiques. His sophisticated style, if not tempered as it was by his pleasant, forthright personality, could have been mistaken as haughty. Their odd partnership initially wrought by Nate's investment capital and Freddy's impecunious situation grew over the years into a full-blown friendship.

Freddy's attitude also brought with it a love of tradition and continuity. This explained why the pre-walk ritual still amused Freddy even though he had witnessed it thousands of times. He boldly commented as only a close friend can without repercussion, "If you keep feeding that dog those franks, he's going to die from high cholesterol."

"You worry too much, Freddy. This dog's

12

mighty and healthy," Nate retorted as he lovingly palmed the now bulging ribs of his best little friend. "We walk at least seven hundred and thirty times a year. Besides, the beer dilutes the cholesterol. Right, Gunner?"

The now sated bulldog immediately emitted a bark as if he precisely understood the comment the old man had made on canine physiology. But now he needed his walk. The brass bell above the front door rang when Nate opened it to lead, or be led, on the second of their twice daily outings.

"If Jo calls, find out if she's still at school. Can you do that for me?"

Not looking up from his book work, Freddy merely nodded saying, "Um uh," as the two stepped onto the brick sidewalk.

~3~

Jack Davidson, the Red Sox owner and one exceptionally tough, savvy businessman, sat behind the expansive walnut desk in his penthouse office. By merely rotating the Italian leather chair, he could look out over Fenway Park and much of the city of Boston as well as Brookline and Cambridge.

But Davidson didn't always feel like turning around, so he merely looked ahead at the giant television that consumed over half of the opposing wall. The closed circuit screen showed his ground crew hard at work prepping the field. Davidson had made his billions by such hands-on observation to insure everything was in order. Unlike most major league owners, he viewed baseball as just another one his enterprises. Baseball for Jack Davidson was totally financial.

Sitting across the desk from him was his latest acquisition, Max Roebuck. Davidson had recently swooped the thirty-eight year old head scout back from the Yankees. Max's scouting talent, especially for hitters, was a direct result of being Nate Lugo's protégé. And all of Baseball considered Nate Lugo the greatest batting coach who ever stepped on a field.

Davidson thrived on owning, controlling and surrounding himself with such attractive, alert individuals. But the lady who sat next to Max Roebuck made Davidson uneasy. She was the organization's head lawyer, Priscilla Courtney. Miss Courtney was Davidson's equal in every respect and on the ethical side, his superior. Her tall, lithe frame impeccably carried her well tailored clothing. This sartorial taste was matched only by her air of Southern culture which was accented by a flowing, articulate North Central Virginia dialect.

Looking up from her copious notes, she confidently stated, "It's all together, gentleman." Then with the ever so slight dropping of the eyes toward her notes, "Except for the wall. Otherwise, we have federal, state, city, and historical approval. All is go." For emphasis, Miss Courtney leaned forward and gestured with her thumb and forefinger less than an inch apart, "We're this close."

Davidson flashed a quick frown, half

ordering, half pleading with his prime legal advisor, "Priscilla, I pay you big bucks. Get me out of this."

"I can't. It's legitimate. Nate Lugo owns the wall."

Davidson leaned back wincing at the plainly stated fact. The wall Ms. Courtney had been referring to was the famed Green Monster, that for decades had given left fielders and hitters alike fits when it came to the strategy in Fenway Park. For the players, it was a factor in the game. For the fans, it had become a symbol of tradition and struggle. For Jack Davidson, it had become an obstacle between himself and hundreds of millions of dollars.

"No way legally to get around it?" he queried.

Miss Courtney continued in her objective, businesslike manner, "It's a simple scenario. When Mr. Lugo was coaching, the owners ran into a cash flow problem. They gave him the wall as a tongue-in-cheek payment with a clause to buy it back within a year. When the club changed owners, the papers got lost in the shuffle, and by the time it was uncovered, it was too late. You've inherited the problem. It was a spoof goof."

Davidson's face immediately reddened and his reaction was the same as always when he could not control. The volume of his voice increased. "To

17

hell with spoof goof. Even in this day and age, business is what it's always been. "War. And you know how I play? "All's fair." *in war."*

Accustomed to such outbreaks, Priscilla Courtney merely looked down and swept an imaginary spot of lint from her skirt. "It's a problem, Jack." *and said*

Davidson nervously rubbed the nape of his neck. "Don't you think I know that? The wall has to go, And quickly It's a black hole sucking my money." Then, somewhat calmer, he turned to Max Roebuck, who up to that point had been attentively listening. "Roebuck, you're in charge. I want that wall."

Blind-sided by this sudden role change and immediate involvement, Max Roebuck quickly responded, "I'm a scout, not a negotiator."

Davidson, stared straight into Max's eyes, stood and leaned toward him, "Become one. Right now, I need that wall. You know that old man better than any of us, so that means you know his weaknesses. I want a bigger ballpark, and I want it now."

On the word *now*, Jack Davidson slammed his fist onto the desk and developed such an intense stare, Max Roebuck thought that he was on fire.

~4~

Roger Gray, Cecil Underwood and Harmon Hudson, each with bat and glove in hand, ran across the (Charles Street) overpass to catch up with three young, very attractive teenage girls. Roger's excitement increased. "There they are."

In his complete preoccupation with the girls, he failed to notice his path would soon cross that of an old man leading an English bulldog. Still watching his would be admirers, Roger ran solidly into Nate Lugo knocking the cigar out of Nate's mouth. Alerted by the error, Cecil, who was closely tailing his friend, avoided the collision by jumping over the leashed Gunner who barked protectively. The lagging Harmon stumbled prompting yet another warning from the four footed protector.

As Nate picked up his cigar, he noticed the gloves and bats. "It's all right, Boy. They're okay."

Harmon picked himself up and smiled at the old man and the dog before yelling to his friends, "Roger. Cecil. Wait up."

By then Roger and Cecil both had already forgotten the incident and once again were concentrating on girl business. Harmon caught up with them once they had slowed to the girl's pace. The boys maintained a safe fifteen foot distance to the rear.

"They're beautiful," said Roger.

"You are absolutely correct, Roger," responded Cecil. "All three are profoundly exquisite."

Still breathing hard from the ordeal, Harmon was once again in sync and on the trail with his buddies. All three girls had long hair and were dressed in perfectly fitting jeans and tops. Roger, Cecil and Harmon followed mesmerized, (not once taking their eyes from the girls' backs.)

"Look at that hair. It's awesome," Harmon gasped. "Do we have any chance at all?"

Still looking ahead, Cecil smiled and answered, "As The Bard so eloquently stated, my dear Harmon, the essence of romance is the uncertainty."

Nothing was uncertain about either the size or the prowess of Sonny Pep. The 205 pound sixteen-year old had a fast ball equaled only by his slider. To the other high school kids, he was a demigod who graced the field only to show them how the game could be played. To boot, his childhood spent in and around his North End neighborhood had equipped him with street smarts that he brought to the field.

Sonny confidently stood on the mound surrounded by his usual team, the North Enders, who seldom lost a pickup game. Each afternoon, weather allowing, from spring to fall they dominated the Charles River ballfield on the Esplanade along the banks of the river. Accustomed to the regular spectators, Sonny reveled in his lordship of the field whenever new faces showed themselves.

Just as the three teenage goddesses sat down, Sonny hurled a steamer down the center of the plate. The batter was still thinking about swinging when it popped the catcher's mitt.

Smiling behind his mask, the catcher side-armed the ball to the first baseman to give the infielders some action taking it around. In a muffled yell shouted, "Strike three. Good arm, Sonny."

The tallest of the three girls, who had caught Roger's eye even more than the other two, leaned toward her friends and in a stage whisper declared, "He's good."

Her shorter but equally pretty Latino friend smiled and lifted her eyebrows. "He's really cute too."

Roger stood within earshot of the girls and pretended to be totally absorbed by the action on the field while taking in every one of the girls' words. The third baseman yelled to the big pitcher as he tossed him the ball, "That's it, Sonny. You've fanned 'em all."

Before he had time to think what he was saying, Roger yelled, "Not all of us."

Everyone near the field seemed surprised at the boldness of the response, none more than Nate Lugo who had stopped to watch the play. All eyes were trained on Roger. Sonny gave his newest challenger the once over, smirked and then extended the *come on* nod to Roger. Knowing there was no turning back, Roger confidently laid down his glove and rubbed his bat.

A wide eyed Harmon loudly whispered, "Are you crazy? You can't hit."

Roger, now at full throttle, started toward the plate. "Nothing ventured, nothing gained."

Cecil looked down at the ground, shook his head and quietly murmured to Harmon, "This should be good."

Roger looked around for one last time before taking his stance and smiled when he saw the girls

watching him instead of Sonny. Reveling in the attention, he winked at them and then faced his impressive foe.

Sonny simply nodded at the catcher's signal, took his windup and hurled a fastball that reached the catcher's mitt before Roger swung. The catcher chortled as he returned the ball to his teammate, "Smokin', Sonny, smokin'.

Roger now knew he was in over his head, but what could he do? The girls were watching. So he looked once again to the mound not planning to be late a second time. He thought Sonny must have lost control because on the second pitch, the ball was speeding toward Roger's head, but not as fast as the first pitch. Just as Roger stepped back, he saw the ball curve down and away from him and in an attempt to redeem himself, he swung completely off balance, evoking laughter from the other players and onlookers alike.

That time the catcher was even more pleased as he spat out a rhetorical question through his grin. "Fooled you didn't he, Wimpy?"

The insult of being called Wimpy was nothing in comparison to the degradation of the girls' laughter. When Roger heard that, he turned to his friends for support, but both Cecil and Harmon merely shook their heads in distress.

The third pitch, a steaming fastball down the

middle of the plate, came so quickly that Roger had no time to swing, considering he had to recuperate from the first two pitches. Nate Lugo looked down at Gunner and commented, "He's gutsy, but he's lousy. Let's go home, Boy."

Roger walked toward Cecil and Harmon passing as close to the girls as possible. His smile was totally ignored as they turned their attention elsewhere. When he reached his two comrades, Roger turned for one more look at the beauties now talking with Sonny Pep.

"They love the way I strike out."

"By *they* I assume you mean the other team," Cecil responded.

"It's all timing and technique," Harmon said. "Timing and technique."

While the three boys gathered their gear and left the Esplanade, Coach Jo Lugo watched from the bench on the South End High ballfield as her players chattered while they practiced. The defense positioned themselves deep as D.A. stepped to the plate and began his pre-batting ritual. First, he hit the cleats of his right shoe with the end of the bat, then his left shoe. Once that was done, he immediately touched the bill of his cap with his right hand, slapped the St. Jude medal around his neck, dropped it further to pull his belt buckle

24

before sliding the hand to the tip of the bat. And then he assumed his stance.

He took the pitch and precisely repeated the ritual. Coach Lugo and all of his team mates were so accustomed that his behavior went unnoticed. Jo stood, clapped, and yelled what had so often become the team's battle cry, "Whatta ya say, D.A.?"

This time the pitch came across the plate letter high and a swing perfected by hours of practice and concentration was unleashed sending the ball high into the air above the overpass and onto the roof of South End High. His admiring team mates all turned to watch the ball sail out of sight. Some shook their heads in disbelief while others stood gaped mouthed or smiling. All admired his talent, but none more than his best friend and future agent who frankly stated, "You're the man, D.A. You're the man."

~5~

after school

Roger Gray and Cecil Underwood walked across the cobblestone street and small grassed park to the front door of the Hudson's home, one of the nineteenth-century brownstones so coveted by so many of the city's dwellers. Cecil was his same old self, but after the previous day's pounding, Roger lacked his usual buoyancy. (the of authority) self-confidence

"Boy, did I ever make an ass of myself yesterday," Roger said as he pounded away on the brass knocker.

"Business as usual," said Cecil in a vain attempt to lend a little levity to the atmosphere.

Before the two could ask why he was not at school that day, an excited Harmon threw open the door. "Hey, guys. In here quick. I got something to show you."

lowly

27

Their curiosity rose as they followed Harmon down the long, beautifully appointed hallway and into his father's well used study. Open books and papers randomly surrounded the large state-of-the-art computer centered on a massive mahogany desk. On each of the three inner walls and between the high windows of the outer wall were shelves packed with volumes on intelligence, evolution and technology. In the corner sitting on a five foot high mahogany podium and overlooking the entire realm was a bust of Charles Darwin illuminated by the afternoon sunlight.

Harmon leaned over behind the desk and opened a wooden crate marked, DR. THEODORE HUDSON- PROPERTY OF M.I.T. INTELLIGENCE LABORATORY. He carefully removed a gray, three lobed helmet with a mirrored face shield. Roger and Cecil's curiosity was even more heightened as they stared at the strange object reflecting the images of the three boys along with the bust of Darwin looking over their shoulders.

"What is that?" asked Cecil.

Harmon smiled and lifted his eyebrows. "Welcome to my world. I worked on this all night and most of today."

Roger was so taken in that he forgot his previous day's exhibition of incompetence. "On what?" he asked.

28

Harmon beckoned them into the hallway. "Come on. I'll show you," he said as he dropped to one knee. ("Help me.") *First, help me.*

The three rolled up the oriental carpets, carefully removed the paintings from the walls and moved them to the parlor opposite the study. Harmon, still beaming, took a tennis ball from his pocket and bounced it as he instructed, "Cecil, come here. Roger, go to the end of the hall."

Both boys did as told. Roger walked twenty-five feet to the other end and turned to face Harmon. Before he could position himself, Roger saw the clumsily tossed ball bouncing down the hallway floor. "Catch," Harmon yelled. The awkward fielding attempt resulted in a missed grounder. "Again," Harmon ordered, not once, but twice as Roger repeated his lackluster performance.

This only heightened the frustration of his previous day's embarrassment. He looked up at the ceiling. "Why am I doing this?" he asked.

"Come on. Don't worry about it," said Harmon leading them back into the study. He sat down at the computer as Roger and Cecil looked on. "Watch," he said as he summoned a green stick figure with a smiling face. In perfectly smooth motions the figure danced across the screen, pivoted, and did front and back flips with equal ease. Roger and Cecil laughed.

"What's that?" asked Roger.

"Who, not what," replied Harmon quickly hitting several keys and the entry button. "Now ask again."

A corrected Roger inquired, "Who's that?"

The green stick figured waved and giggled, "Hi. I'm Razzle Dazzle."

Harmon's excitement caused him to type even faster. "And Razzle is good, Guys. Really good." A three dimensional virtual model of the Hudson hallway appeared. Razzle Dazzle confidently walked to the end of the hallway and assumed the same position Roger had taken only moments before. Harmon pressed the entry button and hit directional keys in an effort to shoot a ball past his virtual nemesis. But Razzle Dazzle easily fielded it. Subsequent shots came fast and furious, but no matter the speed, each was effortlessly handled.

"Cute, Harmon, but so what?" Cecil inquired.

"It's more than cute, Cecil. Razzle is the future. You just met the culmination of bleeding edge technology, a state-of-the-art neurophysiological pattern alteration device." Harmon beamed with pride as he pointed to the screen. "My father's research may be ground breaking, but last night *I* compiled him. No one has ever seen anything like Razzle! Ever. I'll show you." Harmon stood and motioned for Roger take his seat. "Sit here, Roger."

Harmon plugged the helmet into the computer, adjusted it onto Roger's head, lowered the face plate and flipped the *on* switch. "Comfortable?" he asked.

"Strange, but okay," Roger said.

"Time for blastoff. Hang on."

An excited Harmon called up Razzle Dazzle to field the ball from several angles in several positions. Razzle caught the ball off the back wall, fielded it from the ceiling, caught it behind his back off the side wall and easily handled it on the floor. Harmon pressed a key causing the ball's speed to accelerate but Razzle Dazzle easily maintained his activity with a smiling face while Roger's arms, legs and torso lifted and twisted.

Cecil's nervousness finally forced his inquiry. "What's going on, Harmon?"

Harmon could barely contain his excitement. "A new day. That's what's going on. This is awesome."

The two continued to watch Razzle Dazzle develop into a green blur as the speed increased. The now satisfied Harmon hit a key stopping the process. Razzle smiled, walked to center screen, waved and graciously bowed. "Your turn," he said.

Harmon removed the helmet as carefully as

he had put it on and then placed it back into its crate. His attention immediately focused on Roger. "How do you feel?"

"Weird. Really weird." Then he added, "But I kinda like it."

"Come on," Harmon said leading them back into the hallway.

As Roger got back into his previous position, Harmon reached in his pocket. He mischievously smiled and stealthily showed a super ball to Cecil. He turned and flung the ball down the hallway, but unlike before, Roger aptly fielded the much faster ball and casually returned it. Harmon missed the throw, but when he finally chased it down, he tossed it upward and watched as it caromed off the ceiling. The ball ricocheted to the floor and off the back wall with lightning speed. A now elated Roger simply backhanded it and returned the ball with ease.

"Pretty cool, huh?" Harmon asked.

"Yeah," answered Cecil.

"It's only the beginning. Come on." Harmon's enthusiasm continued to grow as he once again motioned them to the study. Once back at the computer, he called up yet another file. This time a film of the famed slugger Mickey Mantle appeared showing his ever threatening, powerful swing.

"That's Mickey Mantle," Harmon explained, "One of the greatest hitters of all time. I downloaded this last night."

Harmon hit a key and the swing repeated. He clicked again and the swing repeated. The third time he clicked, the swing repeated and Razzle Dazzle stepped onto the screen.

"Now let Razzle take over," Harmon said, solely attentive to the process.

On the next three swings, Razzle superimposed himself on Mantle's image and assumed the exact motion. Mantle's image faded until only the moving image of the green figure remained. Razzle smiled as he announced, "Ready for action."

"Oh yeah," exclaimed Harmon turning to his friends. "Now, watch this."

Hitting the keys, Harmon placed Razzle at the plate and hurled a series of pitches, some curves, some fastballs, some knuckleballs, some sliders at ever increasing speeds. Razzle with his Mantle perfect swing hit each as the speed zoomed from sixty, seventy, up to 110 miles per hour.

Harmon once again turned to Roger. "You're up."

The reprogramming went the same as before, but this time the nervousness of all three of the boys was replaced by excitement. The ball became a mere blur as Razzle swung and Roger twitched. The swings, the smile, the wave, and finally Razzle's friendly announcement, "Your turn."

As soon as Razzle gave the go ahead, Harmon removed the helmet and carefully placed it back into the crate before giving his final instruction, "All right, guys. Let's play ball."

~6~

The scene on the North End ballfield was a near duplicate of the previous day. The ball burned into the catcher's mitt as once again Sonny Pep dominated the play. His entourage both on and around the diamond chattered, cheered and took comfort in the business as usual activity.

Even Nate Lugo and Gunner were back standing near the third base line. Gunner turned and tugged at his leash as soon as he saw Max Roebuck, an old friend he remembered from years back. Nate's eyes shot briefly to the side, but as soon as he saw Max, he continued to watch the game as if no one were standing beside him.

"How you doing, Gunner?" Max said as he reached down petting the playful canine, who swayed from side to side on his front paws. Max looked up, "And how you doing, Nate?"

Max's attitude
about baseball
ii Fallen the
money

Nate's reaction was much different than his dog's. "Gunner and I are surviving. You still with that team?" He paused as if searching for some far off answer, "What do they call themselves?"

"You know I'm back with the Sox."

Nate maintained his air of complete disinterest. ("Jo may have mentioned it in passing. Yankees didn't suit you, huh?"

"They were fine. Davidson just offered me a better deal," Max said using his business tone. "I'm the best because I was trained by the best. (That costs. Follow the money. That's the name of the game.")

For the first time in the conversation, Nate recognized his protege. He turned looking straight at the younger man. . "The name of the game is Baseball, Max. Somewhere along the line, you seem to have forgotten that. Or maybe it's the company you're keeping."

"Let's not go there."

"No? So cut the crap. What do you want?"

"I just wanted to touch base with you."

"How did you know I was here?"

"You're predictable."

Both their heads turned instinctively as the crack of a bat sent a long foul ball onto the green of the Esplanade. In the course of their conversation, the two had missed the jeers of players and

36

onlookers alike as Roger Gray once again challenged the North End Monarch.

Sonny smirked at what he considered *lucky wood*. After all, as hard as he threw, any contact was bound to send the sphere sailing. He turned to his fellow North Enders and mocked, "That's the first and last wood of the day. Right guys?"

His players all laughed and began the supportive chatter. Roger stepped back up to the plate. Still maintaining his mocking tone, Sonny grinned, confidently palming the ball behind his back. "Lookie here. One of the Louisburg Sluggers." The unexpected pun evoked laughter that immediately turned to seriousness as Sonny toed the rubber and looked to the catcher for his signal.

The crack of the bat had peaked Max Roebuck's interest. "What about this kid batting?"

"Saw him yesterday," Nate said. "Only he was batting right handed."

Sonny Pep flashed a smile as he saw the catcher's index finger point toward the ground. He went into his windup and in an effort to once again shame a Beacon Hill rich kid, he threw as hard as possible.

But this time, his efforts were not rewarded. The letter high fast ball met with the bat of an altered Roger Gray who with his newly acquired

37

inhabitants
residents

denizens
Pontificating

swing sent the ball rocketing out of the park, across Storrow Drive and towards the open window of a Suffolk University classroom.

Unlike the energetic, interested players on the field, the unsuspecting college students sat lethargically in their classroom wanting to be outside and away from their pontificating professor. The teacher maintained a formal professorial air down to his tie and tweeds which he insisted on wearing during all his lectures despite the warm weather.

very
wordy

"Ladies and gentlemen, awareness of one's environment has never been more important than in contemporary urban society." He waved his hand in a dismissive manner. "Most denizens merely float through life concentrating on," he paused to dramatically emphasize the remainder of his statement, "*who knows what.*"

In a conscious dramatic movement, the professor turned his back on the class and facing the blackboard, histrionically placed one hand over his heart, extended his other palm toward the ceiling and twirled it to indicate a maelstrom that drew in the universal ignorance. He paused before confidently stating, "The elements in their immediate environment totally elude them."

Just as the professor made this move, the ball shot through the window, bounced off his desk, hit

Oblivious to what had just happened, he pipes

the wall and bounced back out the window.

The oblivious talker immediately turned to face a classroom of gaped mouthed students. "You ladies and gentlemen, as my students, must discipline yourselves to a heightened awareness."

Their only response was a speechless stare.

Unused to seeing the other half of his battery battered, the catcher could only respond, "Lucky hit, Wimpy. Dollars to donuts you won't get a piece of the ball from here on."

He squatted and signaled for a curve, which a now angry and somewhat startled Sonny Pep immediately shook off. The smoking fastball burned in a bit lower. For Roger it was the perfect pitch. He stepped into it, and with accurate precision and power blasted the ball toward the same building.

Only this time it lofted onto the roof.

Roger turned and smiled at the catcher. "Got a little piece of that one, didn't I, Wimpy?" Then he confidently turned again and winked at the three girls who had returned to watch *the cute one*. Roger strutted past them, smiled at his buddies and boldly declared, "The girls are back."

Cecil was all grins. "That was great!"

All Harmon could do was agree. "Yeah, man!"

Nate, now more curious than any of the team or other onlookers, had been so absorbed in the spectacle that he hadn't noticed Max leaving. He walked Gunner toward the boys, nodded and addressed Roger. "That was impressive. I once saw a swing like that."

All three were suspicious of the old man. As is usual with many city dwellers, they had frequently seen him, but never really interacted with him. Only Harmon remembered Nate from the collision the day before. He reached down to pet Gunner who lifted his head, snorted and wagged his tail.

"So who am I speaking to?" Nate asked.

"I'm Roger. These are my friends, Cecil and Harmon."

"You boys really like baseball, don't you?"

Even though he was talking to the old man, Roger's attention was still on the three girls. He unabashedly stared at them as he answered Nate's question. "Yeah. Among other things."

Cecil and Harmon were more straight forward and enthusiastic.

"Absolutely," Cecil replied.

"Yeah," Harmon said.

Nate reached in his wallet and pulled out a business card in an effort to command Roger's full attention. Using all the ammunition at hand, he took ~~advantage of the~~ moment. "Stop by my shop tomorrow and we'll talk about putting together a team that will impress all the girls, instead of just one old man."

The three stared intently at the card. Roger looked at the other two and responded, "Sure. Why not?"

"We'll be there," Cecil said.

"You bet," added Harmon.

Nate began walking away. "Say goodbye, Gunner."

Gunner barked a farewell to the boys as the duo started back to the shop finishing their twice daily outing.

North End
South End - No

~7~

Roger, Cecil and Harmon had been thinking about baseball, Razzle Dazzle and Nate Lugo throughout the day, but a busy school schedule prevented any conversations. Now free, they headed down Mt. Vernon and cornered onto Charles Street discussing yesterday's developments.

Harmon was still unclear on the situation. "Why are we going to see this old man?"

"I have a feeling he knows what he's doing," Roger said.

A skeptical Cecil declared, "You have a feeling he can help us get girls?"

"Yeah. So what?" Roger retorted.

The bell above the door rang as the three entered the shop. As usual during that time of day, Freddy was finishing his paper work. "What can I help you with, gentlemen?"

Roger checked himself by looking at the

43

business card. "We're here to see Mr. Lugo."

"At the moment, Mr. Lugo is..."

Before Freddy could finish, Nate yelled from the back room, "Freddy. Are those three boys out there?"

"Yes."

"Send them back."

Freddy closely examined the three. "My, my. Immediate access to the Inner Sanctum. Follow me, gentlemen."

The boys followed Freddy as they meandered around the Chesterfields, brass floor lamps, Shaker tables and stained glass that stood between them and the curtained short hallway that led down two steps into to a back room larger than the showroom. They were overtaken by the rack of neatly arranged bats that circumnavigated the room and defined the space. Above the bats near the ceiling hung caps from all major league teams past and present. Below the caps, the walls were adorned with autographed shirts and photos, many of them with Nate and the game's greatest. The oak framed glass cases that formed a central island contained autographed balls, mitts and gloves. Cleats, tied together, were dispersed throughout. The boys looked around in awe as the ambiance affected them to the point of creating a mysterious feeling of time travel.

Harmon's mouth was wide open. His only comment was "Wow."

"I don't believe this," said Roger. "It's like a museum."

Cecil walked throughout the room looking up, down and around in the vain attempt to take it all in.

Harmon finally got it together enough to ask, "Where did you get all this stuff? Is it real?"

"Most of it's autographed," Nate replied. "Is that real enough for you?"

Freddy smiled the smile of one who knows something others don't. "You have no idea of who you're talking to, do you?"

The boys looked at Nate who in the past thirty seconds had gained their immediate respect as Freddy answered his own question, "Gentlemen, you are now in the presence of Nate Lugo, whom, I might add, many consider the best batting coach of all time."

Still listening, but suddenly distracted, Roger looked directly over Nate at a black and white photo. He stared so intently that Nate felt the top of his balding head thinking Roger had spotted something there. Feeling nothing he turned toward the photo.

"Who's the guy with Marilyn Monroe?" Roger asked.

Harmon smiled at the question while Cecil dropped his head into his hands.

"Wrong question, son. It should be who's the babe with Joe DiMaggio. Only player to ever hit in fifty-six consecutive games."

A chuckling Freddy knew it was time to dismiss himself. "I have an appointment," he announced. "Goodbye, gentlemen. He nodded. "See you tomorrow, Nate."

"Good night, Freddy."

As Freddy walked to the front, Gunner moved toward the boys looking for petting and attention. All three were unable to resist the overtures of the big bulldog. While Roger and Harmon were still scratching and petting him, Cecil turned his attention to the business at hand. "Mr. Lugo, why are we here?"

"That's a fair question, young man." Nate squinted and looked each boy in the eye. "Something's going on that I don't understand. Not yet." Nate nodded toward Roger. "Two days ago you couldn't hit a bull in the butt with a bass fiddle and yesterday I saw a swing I haven't seen in a long time." He paused. "I guess it's time to put our cards on the table."

Nate pulled a Mickey Mantle baseball card from the pocket of his well worn blazer and laid it on the counter. "Does this guy look familiar to you?" He scrutinized each boy's face as he waited for the answer. "If you want me to coach you, I have to know what I'm working with."

The three stared at the card and like criminals caught in the commission of a crime were unable to look up. Cecil finally looked at Nate and then at Roger and Harmon. "He's right."

"It's your call, Harmon," Roger said.

At that very moment Gunner barked as if he knew exactly what was going on. Harmon petted Gunner and then looked at Nate. "I can program any hitter."

Nate leaned back and furrowed his brow. "What do you mean program any hitter?"

Now that the secret was out, Harmon could not contain his excitement. "Yeah. My father works at M.I.T. and he brought home a helmet that I fooled around with and figured out a way to program hitting, catching, throwing, anything. All I need is the film."

Nate put his palm toward Harmon. "Slow down, son," he said. "Let me get this straight." He pointed at Roger. "You made a Mantle out of him?"

Harmon pursed his lips and nodded, "Yeah," then looking around asked, "You got a computer here?"

"There's a new one up front, but I don't know anything about those contraptions. Freddy takes care of all that."

"You don't have to know anything, Mr. Lugo," Cecil proudly commented. "Harmon is to computers what you are to batting."

Roger looked at Harmon. "Go get the helmet. Okay?"

"Yeah. I'll be right back." The still excited Harmon bolted out of the room.

As soon as Harmon left, Roger and Cecil, once again overtaken by the aura of the room, stopped conversing and began investigating all the memorabilia, roaming around the island and perusing the items. Cecil was especially interested in the photos and documents which all contained autographs, some dating back to the nineteenth century. He was closely examining a pair of Ty Cobb's cleats when he noticed a deed framed in green wood hanging below. Predisposed to such matters, his father being the most respected legal negotiator in the city, Cecil was immediately drawn to the document. "Is this real? I mean legal?"

"It's on the up and up. I own it."

An incredulous Cecil responded, "You own the Green Monster? How?"

Roger was now drawn to the document and both boys continued to stare at it as if it contained the answers to all of their needs and desires.

"Back *when*, the front office wanted to keep

me but they ran short of money. So they offered me a piece of the organization. At the end of the day they handed me that." Nate looked up and nodded toward the deed. "The joke was on me. A damn wall." He smiled. "It's not a joke anymore."

"This is worth millions," exclaimed Cecil.

"Young man, "Nate said, "some things in life are more important than money."

Roger couldn't wait to share their new discovery. "Wait'll Harmon sees this," he blurted out.

No sooner had the words come out of his mouth than an even more worked up Harmon rushed through the door carrying the helmet in a black gym bag. When he heard the bell, Nate led the two boys to the front. Gunner followed.

Harmon had already sat down at the computer and was busy setting up the demonstration. Nate stood behind the other two looking on curiously totally unaware he was about to enter a world completely foreign to his experience. His intense concentration turned into a smile when the green stick figure strutted across the screen.

"Say hello to Razzle Dazzle, Mr. Lugo," Harmon said, barely able to contain his own enthusiasm.

Nate was confused. "What?"

Harmon repeated the instructions. "This is Razzle Dazzle. Say hello, Mr. Lugo."

The reluctance came across as nervousness when Nate addressed the smiling green figure. "Hello, Razzle Dazzle."

"Hello, Mr. Lugo," Razzle replied.

Nate laughed causing the others to laugh. Gunner barked three short barks in response to the general gaiety.

Harmon was now in his compete glory. "Razzle can teach the style and form of any major league player to anyone."

Nate frowned. "I don't get it."

"You will," encouraged Harmon. "Sit down." He turned to Roger, half asking, half ordering, "Put the helmet on Mr. Lugo." Then he looked to the now nervous Nate and with complete sincerity requested, "Trust me."

Once inside the helmet, Nate Lugo was introduced to a very familiar world in a very unfamiliar way. The only words he remembered hearing were Harmon's *Here's Mantle.* He quivered at the repeated images of the slugger swinging again and again, and then lifted from his seat as Razzle Dazzle replaced the famed Yankee. Nate watched, twitched and laughed nervously as Razzle swung at a seventy mile an hour pitch, followed by an eighty mile an hour pitch, a ninety, a hundred, a hundred and ten until the green blur caused the nervous tittering to change to euphoric laughter.

Nate Lugo sat in awe, speechless as Razzle came to a halt, but eventually the venerable coach understood beyond the mind and beyond the body to the point of complete internalization. "I've seen this a million times, but I never knew it felt this good." He smiled even broader. "The energy puts timing, technique and form in the backseat. Mickey, you were incredible. Absolutely amazing."

Harmon once again instructed Roger. "Take the helmet off."

As he did, Roger asked Nate, "How do you feel?"

"I love it," Nate immediately responded, "I wish my old bones could take this. How long does it last?"

"Long enough for a ballgame," Harmon answered. "Then we have to reprogram."

A smiling Nate spread his arms gathering in his new found friends and for the first time in years had pure joy in his voice. "Boys, we're going to put together a team of the greatest sluggers who ever lived. We'll even bring them back from the grave. We'll be unbeatable."

The ever practical Cecil made a statement that was more of a question, "But there are only three of us."

The undaunted Nate, now totally infected with Harmon's excitement, immediately replied, "Don't worry about that. I'll get the bodies and Razzle Dazzle will make sluggers out of them. We'll have some team. Are you with me?"

Nate extended his right hand palm down and each of the boys topped the others with his own. Looking up, Gunner stepped into the middle of the circle.

"We're with you, Mr. Lugo," said Roger.

"Coach, fellas. Call me Coach."

All three repeated in unison, "Okay, Coach."

From the screen a smiling Razzle joined in, "Okay, Coach," eliciting laughter from all four and causing Gunner to emit a bark of approval.

~8~

Nate Lugo crossed the outfield at South End High. He watched his daughter in the dugout watching the athletic D.A. at bat. When he got within hearing distance he smiled and yelled so all of her players could hear, "How's it going, Coach?"

Meeting Nate halfway, Jo Lugo threw her arms around her father and gave him a kiss on the cheek. "Hey, Dad. How you doin'?"

Jo's ballplayers and students looked on curiously and protectively as the stranger became immediately intimate with their beloved coach. The infield pulled in close and the outfielders stood frustrated, all wanting to know what was up.

"I got three boys on my side of town looking to play summer ball. I need some ballplayers."

Jo raised her eyebrows. "You back in the game?"

"You bet."

Jo squinted and panned the field shading her eyes with her palm. "I'm a bit short myself. But these seven still want to play and practice."

Nate examined the group of players. "You got to work with what you have."

Joe put a thumb and finger to her mouth, whistled loudly and motioned in the boys. The inquisitive potpourri of Black, Hispanic and White kids gathered round their coach and the intruder.

Once satisfied she had their complete attention, Jo asked, "Are any of you up for summer ball? Let's see a show of hands." Seven hands immediately shot into the air. Jo continued, "This is a commitment on your part. No shirking. You've got a chance to work with a former big league coach." She looked toward her dad and then back at the boys. "Fellas, I'd like you to meet Nate Lugo."

One of the group, Facie Fuller, a chubby African American, spoke up asking the question all the boys were thinking, "Is he kin to you, Miss?"

"He's my dad, Facie, but he also happens to be a former Red Sox batting coach." She proudly looked to her father, "The best who ever stepped on a field."

"We goin' to the majors, Miss?" Facie immediately asked.

This brought laughter to everyone except

54

D.A. and Luther who were standing off to the side.

Nate quickly scanned the whole group and addressed the boys as he would his pro players. "First practice here. Saturday. One o'clock."

Luther Gordon's eyes and hopes dropped as he looked toward the ground. "I can't make it. I work on Saturday."

In a dismissive, matter-of-fact manner, Nate responded, "It's you choice, son. Work or baseball."

Which brought the immediate response from D.A., "If he don't play, I don't play."

An equally fast, stern look was Nate's reply.

Jo motioned her father out of hearing distance of the boys. "Dad, we have to talk." Her look of concern was deep and immediate. She nodded towards Luther. "If he doesn't work, he doesn't eat. Some of these boys are on their own. I don't know what you have in mind, but this could be the best thing in their lives."

Looking into his daughter's caring eyes, Nate began to realize his error. Pondering the situation, he looked over at the boys and this time instead of ballplayers, he saw the faces of working class and underclass kids looking to him for guidance. The top shelf athlete D.A. and his aspiring agent, Luther Gordon. Racie Fuller, the ever inquisitive kid always asking the questions everyone else wished they had the guts to ask. Frizz Stephens, a tall, dark skinned, emotional Jamaican who was usually all smiles and always ready for harmless mischief. Ray Leveroni, half Italian and half Cree Indian, who had the habit of shuffling from foot to foot while constantly and nervously pounding his glove. Stretch McCabe, the tall red headed Irish kid, the stoic of the group, And Harold Chavez, the small, well-built, feisty but respectful Hispanic with thick, dark, curly hair.

"All right guys," Nate said, "first practice here Sunday at one o'clock. Don't be late."

Jo smiled, pleased to see her father once again involved in her life as well as in baseball. The boys were all excited about the prospects of summer ball with a big league coach, but as is common among their age group, they didn't want to show it.

As an equally pleased Nate Lugo started toward his car, he noticed Max Roebuck watching in the distance.

~9~

It was almost midnight in the Inner Sanctum when Nate finished his carefully devised plan that would stun the baseball world. He sat at a table covered with green felt. The overhead lamp lent a hazy, dreamlike ambiance to the surrounding baseball memorabilia. The only sound in the room came from across the table top where Gunner stood lapping beer.

Nate looked down for a final once over of the nine cards he had carefully chosen and uniformly placed on the felt. He reached over and patted his trusted confidant. "These are the players, Gunner." He emitted a self satisfied, "Ha," and further explained, talking to both himself and his dog, "The greatest team of hitters ever assembled. All of them hall of famers except Rose. It's a coach's dream."

Nate leaned back in his chair and looked at

the impressive array of the images of Mickey Mantle, Joe Dimaggio, Babe Ruth, Ty Cobb, Pete Rose, Lou Gehrig, Willie Mays, Ted Williams and Hank Aaron.

"What do you think of this team, Boy?"

Gunner's bark caused him to laugh, but the laugh faded into the lone night air as Nate Lugo walked behind the high desk and removed his deed from the wall.

"It's a tough call. I'm risking a lot to get back in the game, but who knows? Maybe the old man still has a few things to teach those kids."

He carried the deed back to the table and alternately looked at it and the images on the nine cards. Finally he laid down the document, turned his full attention to the cards and with no doubt in his voice said, "Let's do it."

Smiling inside and out, Nate Lugo proudly exclaimed, "There they are, Gunner. The Louisburg Sluggers."

~10~

S unday brought not one but four new faces to
the South End ball park. Five if you were to
count Gunner, who lapped up all the attention
paid to him no matter which way he turned. But *then*
even Gunner's popularity gave way to the curiosity *what was*
in Harmon's hefty laptop and the strange object he *was*
carried with him in the black bag. *enclosed*

Nate introduced the Beacon Hill three, then
immediately got down to business. "Guys, listen
and listen strong. Harmon here is in charge of
training." He pointed toward the black bag. "This
helmet will make all of you better players, but if the
word gets out, it's worthless. It's our secret, and
we've got to keep it. Understood?"

Nate's tone combined with the street smarts
of the South End group allowed the intended
impression to be made. From that time on each of
them knew if the secret leaked, they would lose. But

59

none of them was yet aware of how much.

He stared at each of the boys to reinforce the gravity of his statements. Satisfied his point had been driven home, Nate said, "Show 'em how it works, Harmon."

Curiosity heightened as the group intently watched Harmon place the helmet on Roger and start the process.

"Who's that green guy?" asked Facie when Razzle appeared on the screen.

"Tell him, Razzle," instructed Harmon.

"Razzle looked at the expectant admirers, smiled and boldly greeted them. "Hi. I'm Razzle Dazzle."

Everyone including Nate and Jo burst into laughter as the energetic green figure waved, smiled and walked across the screen. But the laughter soon changed to serious, rapt attention when the image of Mickey Mantle appeared followed by Razzle's superimposition and Roger's twitching. By the time Harmon removed the helmet and Roger started toward the plate, not a sound was uttered.

Jo Lugo took her place behind the L screen on the mound and began throwing. The ability of the former All American was evident. She threw hard, fast and accurately. But Roger hammered the first pitch and every strike thereafter until the bucket of balls was entirely empty. Harmon smiled at his handiwork as he watched the group of players who were seldom ~~that~~ quiet for that long. Each stood captivated by the performance but none more so than D.A.

Nate stepped forward and called for attention. "All right, fellas. You got the idea. I've picked the nine best sluggers I could come up with. He held up eight carefully folded slips and dropped them into his cap. "Roger's already been programmed to Mantle, so the rest of you choose now." He raised the cap within reach.

Luther elbowed his way to the front, "Let me go first."

Nate moved the cap over Luther's head as the would-be agent fingered the first chit and handed it to Nate. "Who are you," Nate asked?

"Luther Short."

"Now you're Joe DiMaggio. Who's next?"

"Me. Frizz Stephens."

Nate had to hold the cap higher as the excited Jamaican pulled his counterpart. "Ty Cobb, one of the best," Nate said putting the hat over Cecil's head. "Draw, Cecil." Nate smiled as he read. "Pete Rose. Hustle and consistency. Good choice."

Nate walked over to the red head, who would have never stepped forward on his own. "What's your name, son?"

"Stretch."

"Go for it, Stretch." Stretch McCabe gave an uncharacteristic smile as he handed the note to Nate who looked pleased when he revealed, "Willie Mays. The Say Hey Kid." Nate smiled at the curly headed Hispanic. "And you are?"

"Chavez."

"Get in here, Chavez."

Unlike the others, Chavez frowned and handed the paper back to Nate. "I don't want to be Lou Gherig," he emphatically stated.

The response surprised Nate. "Why not?"

"I want to be Roberto Clemente."

"I didn't choose Clemente."

"Why not? He wasn't great?" Chavez asked staring directly into his new coach's face.

"I think Gehrig was better'" Nate argued. "He had 300 more hits and double the home runs."

Chavez quickly retorted, "Roberto Clemente was a great player. He was a good guy too. And I'm a good guy, I want to be Clemente."

Nate pondered the situation as he stared back into the dark unflinching eyes of Harold Chavez. "Okay, kid. Today you're Gehrig. Next practice, we'll program Clemente." Nate looked at the rest of the team with a stern resolve. "But that's it. No more replacements. Got it?"

Facie Fuller nodded and looked up. "I'm Facie."

"Pick one, Facie."

The baby face smiled as he handed Nate his pick and awaited his new identity. His smile got even bigger at Nate's enthusiastic response, "You're the man, Facie. The Bambino. The Sultan of Swat. Babe Ruth."

"Yeah, Babe Ruth," repeated Facie as he pivoted and started to the dugout awaiting his turn to be programmed.

Nate checked the list he was holding. "Next draw, Leveroni." Leveroni's hand shook as he returned the slip. "You're Hammerin' Hank Aaron, the Home Run King." Nate nodded his approval and smiled. A return nod every bit as strong indicated Leveroni's approval as well.

Without looking Nate handed the last slip to D.A. "That leaves Ted Williams. Can't do much better than that, kid."

Like Leveroni, D.A. nodded his approval.

It was a satisfied Nate Lugo who turned to Harmon Hudson and yelled, "Hook 'em up, Harmon. We got practice."

That day, each of the South End High players experienced what Roger had felt only days earlier. The spirit of technology was fused with the souls of the streets as each boy took on his alter-identity. That practice and subsequent ones brought with them the excitement of their new beings along with the joy of playing at an ultimate level, but as is so often the case, they also brought with them ugly realities.

~11~

Over the course of the next five weeks, the tedium of school, especially springtime school, came to an end and both the South Enders and the Louisburg trio settled in for the much anticipated Boston summer. The four practices a week continued, and fortunately Boss, the owner of the Elizabeth Diner where Luther Gordon, Stretch McCabe and Frizz Stephens worked, was a die-hard baseball fan. Because of that, they were able to attend all practices.

To the casual observer, the practices would seem ideal. When the boys were not programmed, Nate and Jo taught them the basics of the game; base running, fielding and field shifts, glove work and batting tips. Even Gunner contributed by gathering balls and toting them to the practice bucket, but of course, he expected to be rewarded with beer.

During all this activity, little escaped Nate Lugo's expert eye and years of hard earned experience, and with that he became acutely aware of a clash of the classes. Subtle indicators like the lack of verbal support or teamwork soon gave way to direct confrontations. At one point Ray Leveroni squared away against Cecil Underwood when the latter slid under a throw, safe at second. The skirmish would have developed into an all out brawl if the cool-headed, business-minded Luther Gordon had not stepped between them.

Nate observed the incident, but decided to stay out of it as long as possible and let the boys develop their own team spirit. Still his doubts concerning the differences increased to the point that he had to question his own abilities with his daughter.

"Can we make this happen?" he asked.

"They're kids, Dad. Just kids. We'll make it happen."

On the other hand Roger Gray had no misgivings whatsoever. As time went by the number of girls watching the practices was growing even greater. First three of the South End girls, probably friends or sisters of his teammates, came on a regular basis. Then six. Then eight. Then a whole section of them joking, laughing, doing one another's hair, exchanging cosmetics, the things girls that age do. That is when they weren't checking out the guys.

Baseball and girls. Girls and Baseball. Roger Gray loved every minute of it.

But frequently, another onlooker, not unnoticed by Jo and Nate, would appear among the locals as he watched from the outfield or hovered in the bleachers in his attempt to discover what Harmon was doing in the dugout. On one such occasion when Max Roebuck was sitting by himself on the top row, Nate knew it was time to talk. He casually walked up the concrete aisle and sat beside Max on the metal bench.

"You like what you see?" asked Nate.

Max casually placed his foot on the bench in front of him. "Not bad," he replied, knowing well his old mentor was up to something. "What's going on?"

"I've got a proposition for your money people."

The statement instantly turned Max's head. "I'm listening."

"I want a game."

This furthered Max's curiosity. "What kind of game?"

"My boys here against the Sox."

Max gazed down at his shoes, then back at Nate. "Against the Sox?"

Nate nodded.

"Whatta we talking? Three innings of light baseball?"

"Nine innings. Straight out. My kids can win."

Nate's statement had not fully soaked in before Max impulsively asked, "What are you crazy?"

"I got a wall."

Now it did soak in. At that moment Max Roebuck felt like the luckiest man alive. Here was the object of his goal handed to him on a plate. Still a bit in disbelief, he asked the reinforcing question, "You're willing to risk the wall?"

Nate looked at his daughter and the boys, now *his* boys, on the field as he spoke, but he seemed to be in another time, maybe another place. (The deal is, if we win, the park stays and the wall is left even if a new stadium is built around it.) Damn, Max, I know things have to change, but that doesn't mean completely turning your back on the past." He fixed his eyes on his protege. "You got to look back once in a while to know where you're going."

The advice slid past Max. "And if we win, we get the wall? No strings attached?"

"You got it."

"I'll get you a meeting." Max smiled and extended his hand.

~12~

Jack Davidson and Priscilla Courtney both knew when Max Roebuck called an emergency evening meeting something important was in the air. Like his mentor, Max was not one to exaggerate.

And Jack Davidson didn't like to beat around the bush either. "So he wants a deal?"

"Nope," said Max. "He wants a game."

Davidson leaned back in his leather chair and snatched the ball signed by Babe Ruth himself from its desk stand. As he was prone to doing, he nervously tossed it from palm to palm and asked, "What kind of game?"

"The kids I told you about. Against the Sox. For the wall."

Davidson stopped tossing the ball and waited for Max to deliver the punch line. For a brief moment, the silence could not have been louder.

Until Jack Davidson broke it. He slapped the

ball into his left palm, stood and began meandering about the office. This served to accentuate the movement of stomach caused by the silent mocking laugh. He walked behind Max, leaned over his shoulder and went into a diatribe that was part question, part sermon, "Play a bunch of kids?" He leaned even closer and whispered in Max's ear, "That's ridiculous. We're pros." A pause punctuated his next statement. "As in professional. You do remember that word, don't you?" Davidson stood erect, walked in front of Max and stared down. "This is about money, Roebuck. It's not a game."

Max wanted to say *Yes it is, And the name of the game is Baseball.* But instead he lowered his eyes.

Davidson tossed the ball even harder as he began thinking out loud. "Our guys against a bunch of kids. That old man's gone over the edge. He's really out there."

Priscilla Courtney, who had so far remained calm and silent, made a simple statement, "We could disguise it as a charitable event, Jack dear. Great for public relations, And you get your wall."

Max's eyes lit up. "She's right. It's a win-win situation."

Now realizing the potential and again realizing why he paid Priscilla Courtney the big bucks, Davidson began to settle down. He calmly placed the ball back onto its stand. "That damn Green Monster." He looked at Max. "Set up a meeting."

Max left immediately and in fifteen minutes was inside Yesterday's News. Freddy, who had a late appointment with a client, was preparing for it at the front desk when Max rang the bell.

He greeted Max in his usual formal manner. "Mr. Roebuck."

"Hi, Freddy. Is Nate here?"

Freddy yelled to the back, "Nate, Someone to see you."

Max began looking around at the old, expensive items and made his way to the hallway peering toward the Inner Sanctum. When Nate emerged through the curtain, Max caught a glimpse of the bats, cleats and shirts.

"Still living in the past, Nate?"

"It's better than your world," Nate responded. "You got something for me?"

"Yeah. A meeting."

"When?"

"Noon tomorrow," Max replied using his most businesslike tone. "Bring your lawyer."

"We used to strike a deal with a handshake."

Max extended his hand to seal their part of the bargain.

"See you tomorrow," Max said.

"I'll be there. So will my lawyer."

Satisfied with a good day's work, Max Roebuck skipped once as he heard the bell above his head heralded him out the door. If he were younger, he would have run down Charles Street.

While the short conversation between Max and her father was occurring, Jo Lugo had pulled her car across the street from Yesterday's News. As she did, she noticed a dark sinister looking character staring at the shop through black sunglasses. Just as Max skipped out the door, the imposing figure turned his head to reveal a scorpion tattoo on the side of his neck just below his right ear. His creepiness was magnified by the setting. He in no way fit the Beacon Hill mold. Jo shuddered a bit and then followed the motion of the stranger's turning head to catch a glimpse of Max leaving the shop. When she looked back, the stranger had vanished.

Jo crossed Charles Street as Freddy was turning the OPEN sign to CLOSED. She tapped on the window and smiled. Freddy opened the door and on the run kissed her cheek. "Hi, Jo. Bye, Jo. Will you lock up after me?"

Smiling with a *that's Freddy* attitude, Jo replied, "Sure thing. Bye."

After locking the door, Jo made her way into

the Inner Sanctum to find her father staring down at the green felt table. "I just saw Max leaving," she said, breaking Nate's intense concentration. "What did he want?"

Nate started. He quickly glanced up, but avoided direct eye contact before placing the deed back in its place on the wall. There were a lot of things Jo Lugo did not know about life, but she did know one thing. Jo Lugo knew her father.

"I'm not believing this," she burst out.

"What are you talking about?"

"You know what I'm talking about. You're gambling again. That's what I'm talking about."

"Look Jo, it's..."

"Don't look Jo me. I'm not a little girl anymore."

With that statement, Jo's admonition turned to hurt and fear.

Nate immediately reacted to the look in his daughter's eyes. "It's not like that."

"Yes it is, Dad. You put Mom through it. I saw it." Jo's open palm went down cutting the air between her and her father. "I saw it all first hand."

At this tears began to form in her eyes, Nate walked over, took his daughter's hand and led her to the chair beside his. "Sit down, Jo. It's all right. It's different this time."

"No." Jo shook her head side to side. "No.

Gambling is gambling. It's dangerous and you know it."

"Sit down, Jo," Nate said. "No arguing. Please."

They both sat facing one another. Nate leaned forward, reached out and held Jo's hands. "Since your mother died, things have been very different for me. I don't live. I survive." He paused reflecting on his last statement. "I don't mean I'm not grateful, but it's just day to day. (You and Gunner are all I have left of your mother.) Nate leaned even closer. "She loved you so much, and she was so proud of you." Nate reached over and petted Gunner. "She loved this dog too. When she bought him, she said he reminded her of me. So damned ugly, he was cute."

At that, both Jo and Nate laughed, but through the laughter Jo noticed the tears in her father's eyes. "Other than your mom and you, I only believe in three things; God, Gunner and The Game. I've got two of them now, but it's not enough. I'm not a whole person. I need The Game, Jo. Those kids have given me the chance to live again." Nate leaned down very close to his daughter's face looking deeply and earnestly into her eyes. "Understand?"

Jo looked back at her father and took a moment to absorb the conversation before replying,

"It's dangerous."

"Life's a risk, Jo. This time it *is* for The Game. You've got my word on it." Nate lifted his arm palm forward into an oath taking position. "I swear on your mother's grave."

"Those kids sure as hell better come through."

"They will," Nate said. "I know character when I see it." He smiled, reached down and petted Gunner. "Besides, Gunner okayed it. Right boy?"

The reply was a loud affirmative "Woof."

Fifteen year old —
Beth Underwood =

~13~

Priscilla Courtney and Max Roebuck were already seated at the conference table when the receptionist announced over the intercom that Mr. Lugo and Mr. Underwood were there to see Mr. Davidson. All three were surprised when Nate Lugo stepped into the office followed by a fifteen year old. Both Max and Priscilla stood but Davidson remained seated and like Facie Fuller asked the question the other two wanted to ask, "Who's the kid?"

"He's my agent," said Nate.

"He's a kid," snapped Davidson.

"I didn't tell you how to choose your lawyer, Davidson." Nate flashed a warm smile in Priscilla's direction. "But I must admit if I did, I would seriously consider this lady. Nate Lugo, Ma'am," he said extending his hand.

Priscilla Courtney delicately offered her hand and in a professional manner responded, "So this is the famous Nate Lugo I've been hearing about. Miss Priscilla Courtney, Mr. Lugo."

"My pleasure, Miss Courtney."

At this point Cecil stepped forward and introduced himself. "Cecil Underwood, Miss Courtney."

"You appear to be a gentleman like your father. How is he?" she asked shaking Cecil's hand.

"Quite well, thank you."

Jack Davidson incredulously piped in, "You know his father?"

"I've known Bart Underwood for years," Priscilla said. "He's well known in legal circles. Quite the negotiator."

The familiarity compounded the already uncomfortable situation for Davidson, so he responded in his usual manner. He took control. "Enough of this father-son crap. Let's get down to business."

As the four seated themselves, Cecil reached into his briefcase and pulled a folder filled with documents. Priscilla's eyes were fixed on her legal pad. She looked up. "Gentlemen, it's time to define the terms."

Cecil immediately responded, "If you don't mind, I've taken the liberty to draw up a contract

Gumore

which I believe you'll see is in order. The terms are clearly stated." He distributed five copies to the others who intently began perusing them.

After quickly scanning the document and taking in the germane information, an acute skill that had enabled him to form his empire, Davidson asked Priscilla, "How does this look?"

"Straight forward and concise," she answered. "Proper legal format."

Cecil looked directly at Davidson. "It's really quite simple. (We want the specified equipment and uniforms of our own design. All pro."

Still looking at the contract Davidson responded, "No problem."

Cecil continued, "As previously agreed by Mr. Max Roebuck and Mr. Nate Lugo, if the Red Sox should win, Mr. Lugo relinquishes all rights to the green wall in the left field of Fenway Park to Mr. Jack Davidson."

At that, Davidson looked up and smiled.

Cecil continued, "Should the Louisburg Sluggers win, the green wall remains where it is under the ownership of Mr. Nate Lugo and any new park will be built around it."

"Agreed," said Davidson. His smile broadened.

Cecil, barely able to hide the pride of his meticulous research, read the next term. "Also, as stated in Section III, if the Louisburg Sluggers should win, three townhouses in the new Bellingham Development will be donated, (fee simple,) to the families of Luther Short, Facie Fuller and Harold Chavez."

"Sure, kid," Davidson said and with an infrequent hint of respect, raised his eyebrows and nodded. He turned to Priscilla. "Anything else?"

Priscilla pulled a sheet from under her legal pad. "Everything so far is in order, but we need to cover one more detail. We can add it as Section IV," she said looking at Cecil. "Considering this is a charitable event, Mr. Davidson has agreed to give a twenty-five thousand dollar donation to the Jimmy Fund should the Red Sox win. Should the Louisburg Sluggers win, Mr. Davidson will donate one million dollars to the same charity."

Cecil smiled at the prospect of another bonus as he added it to the contract. Nate leaned back in his chair. "That's mighty noble of you, Jack."

Davidson impatiently stood. "Looks like we're done." He focused on his attorney. "We're through?"

Priscilla nodded her approval. Once the two principals had signed, she handed Max a pen. "Here, Mr. Roebuck. You be the witness."

Throughout the entire process Nate had found it difficult to keep his eyes off the attractive attorney. Now that business was over, he could devote his full attention to her. He stood and half nodding, half bowing, said, "It's been a pleasure, Ma'am. Hope to see you again soon."

Priscilla smiled. "I'm sure you will." by soon

Davidson broke the moment. "And I'll see you on the Fourth, Lugo. Don't forget the deed."

Nate ignored the remark and leaned toward Max. He smiled and whispered, "You were quiet."

"Not a lot to say."

Nate nodded. "You take care."

Max nodded back at Nate and then at Cecil as the two left the office making their way back home to Beacon Hill.

~14~

The South End ballpark pulsed with the sounds of practice. Coaxing, teasing and laughter interrupted the sounds of bats hitting balls and balls hitting gloves in the fast pepper warmups. The entire team was busy doing what boys do best. Play.

Nate's whistle cut through the air gaining the attention of the chattering players. They immediately became quiet. He motioned them towards the dugout. "Come on in, fellas. Hustle up." As soon as the group assembled around him, he looked to Cecil. "Everybody here?"

Cecil stood on the bench and took a speedy head count. "All accounted for."

Nate purposely paused and slowly looked at each of the boys to heighten the tension. "What are your plans for the Fourth?"

"I have to work," said Luther.

"I'm at the beach," smiled Roger looking around at the other boys. "Girls galore."

Roger's remarks set off a hubbub of laughter interspersed with comments about fireworks and bonfires. A series of louder, fragmented conversations quickly developed among the boys. Nate held his hand high over his head, whistled again and then yelled above the din, "How about a game in Fenway Park?"

They were stunned. Silence blanketed the boys.

"Quit playing us, Mister," Facie finally said.

"I'm not," Nate replied. He turned to Cecil. "Tell 'em."

As if delivering a gift to equal that of the Magi, Cecil stepped onto the bench and announced in his most serious tone, "Two o'clock. On the Fourth of July, Fenway Park, Against the Red Sox."

An eerie calm consumed the next few seconds. Then all the boys exploded at once into a joyous frenzy, jumping up and down, hugging one another and high-fiving.

Nate let them have their moment before adding to it, "If we play in the pros, we got to look like the pros. Everybody to the bus. We're getting uniforms and gear."

As the kids vied for the window seats on

Davidson's hired bus, their good fortune began to soak in.

The outfitter at the pro shop, not used to seeing such a young clientele, carefully scrutinized the group as Nate and Jo walked in with ten teenagers and a dog. Gunner boldly approached the stranger who immediately kneeled and petted his new found friend. He smiled and looked up. "You must be Nate Lugo."

Nate nodded and extended his hand. "I understand you're the one to fit us with practice and game uniforms. Caps, cleats, bats, gloves, the whole schmear." He smiled when he added, "On Jack Davidson's account."

"No problem." The outfitter walked behind the counter and picked up his order pad. "Who's the team?"

Nate reached in his folder and took out a sheet with the logo the boys had designed and agreed upon. He smiled as he proudly slapped it on the counter. "This is our logo and colors. We're the Louisburg Sluggers."

In a mere three days the game and practice uniforms were delivered to the South End field along with a new glove, two pair of cleats, two warmup jackets, a half dozen undershirts, six caps, three pairs of batting gloves, two pairs of sunglasses, a dozen pairs of socks, and even jocks and cups for each boy. When the overall team's six dozen bats, weight rings, and two gross of balls were added to this, the delivery truck was filled.

The team looked like a big family at Christmas unloading and opening the packages, putting on the uniforms, hitting the palms of new gloves, trying on cleats and testing the heft of the new bats. Even Nate Lugo felt like a kid again when he slipped on his new team jacket.

At that moment, for all concerned, happiness ruled.

Jo was collecting open boxes and wrappers in her effort to keep the festivities under control when she looked up to see two familiar figures striding across the outfield. She dropped her armload and rushed toward them. "Uncle Clyde. Uncle Billy," she exclaimed, with an excitement and fond familiarity cultivated by years of warmth. Nate's two contemporaries responded in-kind giving Jo hearty hugs. "It's great to see you," she said.

As he hugged his adopted niece, Billy Ray Block glanced up to see his old friend and colleague sporting a new royal blue jacket. Like Nate, the old school announcers had a deep intrinsic love and respect of The Game that they showed inside and out.

Both Billy Ray and Clyde Gooding were dressed like they had just stepped out of a 1940s movie. No sweatpants and tee shirts for those two. For them, seersucker suits, linen sportcoats, spectator bluchers and Lisle cotton shirts defined casual. Clyde was wearing his ever present trademark, a fine Optimo straw hat that he sported from Memorial Day to Labor Day at which time he donned one of his fifteen beaver felts.

"Glad you could make it," said Nate. "How you boys doing?"

"None the worse for wear, you old war-horse," answered Clyde. "A bit slower than I used to be. How about you?"

"I'm ready to play."

"Yeah? And we're ready to get behind the mic again," said Billy Ray.

Jo sensed it was time to dismiss herself. "I need to help these kids, so I'll get out of your way," she said walking back to the team.

Still waving at Jo, Clyde asked, "So what's going on, Nate?"

"I have a game on July Fourth. Against the Sox."

Clyde beamed. "A charity game. Sounds like fun."

Nate's tone indicated anything but fun. "We're playing to win."

Billy Ray slightly extended his neck in response to Nate's definitive statement. "You're kidding, right?"

Clyde looked into Nate's completely serious face. He removed his hat and casually wiped the sweatband with his handkerchief. "You crazy son-of-a-gun. You're serious, aren't you?"

"I never kid about baseball. Come to the game and announce for us," Nate said. "You've waited your whole lives for this one. That's why I called you." He paused before adding, "Trust me."

Through decades of experience, Clyde and Billy Ray both had learned that Nate Lugo would do his best to deliver, Or die trying.

"We're there, Nate. Right, Billy?"

"I'm up for it," Billy answered. He looked at Nate. "I hope you have strong pitching. The Sox are hitting better than they have in a long time."

Nate suddenly realized a grievous, obvious and possibly fatal error. He had been so myopic in his forte that he had forgotten the most important of the defensive elements. Pitching. "We'll manage," he said.

"We're all set then," said Clyde, "and we're close enough to Packy's and it's close enough to four to catch a bite and a beer. You coming, Nate?"

"Thanks, fellas," Nate said but his mind was elsewhere. "I may catch you later."

As Clyde and Billy Ray casually made their way across the field, Nate quickly made his way toward the bench. Jo immediately picked up on his intense movement and the confused look on his face. "What's wrong, Dad?"

"I screwed up. I got carried away with the sluggers. We need a pitcher." Nate looked to Jo. "What do we do?"

"No problem, Dad" Jo said. "I've got your pitcher. He'll only need one practice."

"Who is it?"

She smiled. "It's a surprise. I've got some footage for you to see."

~15~

move to end

Nate sat in front of the television in his daughter's apartment sharing a beer with Gunner and waiting for the answer to his oversight. He felt embarrassed about such an omission at his age. It's the type of error he would expect one of his teen players to make, But not Nate Lugo. *Maybe I am getting too old,* he thought.

A much more calm and confident Jo Lugo placed a tape with the handwritten label, *The King and His Court,* into the VCR. She sat down beside her father.

Billy Ray's comment earlier in the day had caused Nate's confidence to plummet. For the first time since meeting the Beacon Hill boys, he was low. In his own mind, he questioned if he made other oversights that could cause problems. "I don't know, Jo. This could be a tough team to keep together. They're a motley group."

"So are the Sox, Dad," she said in a matter of fact manner. "One step at a time. Watch this." Jo pushed the play button. Action shots of the greatest softball pitcher ever to toe a rubber appeared on the screen. "Remember Yakima Softball Camp?" Jo's smile indicated perfect self-satisfaction. "There he is, Dad. My mentor. Eddie Feigner. Fastest pitcher on record. He was clocked at 114 miles per hour."

Nate leaned forward and focused on the expert pitcher effortlessly burning the ball across the plate. With each pitch, the old batting coach developed a deeper appreciation for the yet older phrase *firing the ball*.

"He won 8,070 of his 10,000 games using only a four man team. *The King and His Court*," Jo chuckled. "Look at him, Dad. 238 perfect games. 930 no-hitters. Over 1900 shutouts with 132,000 strikeouts. Whew." She leaned towards Nate, mimed a cigar and raised her eyebrows ala Groucho Marx. "Not bad, huh?"

Nate sat back and took a sip of his beer. "Remember that exhibition in Dodger Stadium. Feigner fanned Mayes, McCovey, Robinson, Wills, Killibrew and Clemente all in a row?"

Jo smiled and nodded. "Same thing again with Aaron, Mays, Mantle and Williams in the Astrodome." Both father and daughter smiled as they watched the smooth, powerful underhand delivery. "They all had trouble with his rising fastballs and sliders. Those curves broke eighteen inches." Jo switched off the tape. "Well, Dad. Do we have a pitcher?"

Nate smiled like the cat that ate the canary. "I'll take this tape to Harmon tonight," he said. He stood and raised his hand for Jo to clasp. "Pure genius. I raised a genius."

~16~

The next day at the South End ballpark Nate sat on the bench next to Harmon just as he finished programming the players. The unsuspecting youth looked up from his work and peered over his glasses. "Hi, Coach."

"Are you ready to pitch?" asked Nate. Harmon's mouth fell open. "Come on, Science Boy. It makes sense. You're the only one who isn't programmed."

Harmon stood and started pacing back and forth. "Me? No way, no how." Harmon emphasized his dissension by wildly flailing his skinny arms. "I'm a geek. A brainiac. I can barely walk let alone pitch to the majors." Harmon's brow furrowed and his declarations turned to pleas. "Don't do this to me, Coach."

Nate looked at the anxious desperation in

Harmon's young eyes, sympathetically nodded and agreed, "Okay."

For the first time in his short life, Harmon Hudson was a power athlete. His underhand delivery was so smooth and powerful that even D.A. batting as Ted Williams was behind the pitches. Harmon struck him out, spread his arms to their complete width and strutted around the mound like a bantam rooster.

"How good am I?" he boasted. "The best you've ever seen. Am I right?"

That didn't set too well with the South Enders. It burned them all, especially Frizz and Ray. During the past two practices they had reached their limits with the steadily building tension. Cecil shook his head in disbelief as he rushed to follow Roger to the mound. Both stood their ground with Harmon as Roger supportively slapped his friend on the shoulder. "Harmon. Why are you acting this way?"

"What? I got it. Right? I'm smokin' em all." Harmon turned and panned the field. "Who's up?" He reached down and grabbed dirt. "Next."

"You gotta calm down," Roger said.

Overhearing the comment, Frizz yelled, "You better calm him down or we will."

Roger jumped to Harmon's defense. "It's his

first time. Give the guy a break."

"Yeah. As in break his head," Leveroni said.

Sensing trouble, D.A. ran toward the mound.

"Head as in brains," Roger said. "Without those brains we wouldn't be playing in Fenway."

Harmon with his new found confidence added, "Yeah. Brains are cool. Can you understand that?"

The question was too much for Frizz Stephens to take. He started for Harmon with blood in his eyes. "Ain't nobody gonna call me stupid."

D.A. was able to bear hug Frizz from behind while Roger stepped directly in front of Harmon in a last ditch effort to prevent a team brawl. The rest of the boys began barking out fighting words and moving toward the mound. Hearing the commotion, Nate and Jo rushed from behind the backstop.

That afternoon the Louisburg Sluggers witnessed something none of them had ever seen. An angry Nate Lugo.

"That's it," Nate yelled. "No fightin' on my field." He pointed toward his daughter. "We leave for two minutes and this is what happens?" His words became sharper and louder. The message was brief and clear. "Practice is over. Pack up your gear and get out of here."

The boys stood frozen. None of them uttered

a sound. Nate took off his cap and whacked it against his leg. That wasn't enough so he looked down and kicked the dirt as hard as he could. "I'm not believing this. The last practice before the game and you guys decide to fight. I don't need this. I really don't need this. I need a team."

Nate looked at the two leaders. "D.A. Roger. Get over here. Now."

Nate turned his back and quickly walked away. D.A. and Roger obeyed. When he was a sufficient distance from being overheard, Nate stopped and still looking at the ground motioned for them to stand in front of him.

"You two square this away." His voice was quiet, but never stronger. "If you can't play as a team, you may as well not show up tomorrow." With that said Nate Lugo turned his back on all of them and walked away. The boys stood speechless for a moment and then, still not saying anything, began gathering their gear.

"I don't believe this either," said Jo. "My dad risked all he has left of baseball for you guys and you can't even play as a team. He told me he had complete faith in your character and this is what you give him." She turned to follow her father. "Maybe he was wrong."

Jo Lugo, the Beacon Hill three and the South Enders all left in different directions.

~17~

L uther Gordon, Stretch Ramone and Frizz Stephens entered the Elizabeth Diner showing off their new Louisburg Sluggers jackets. The regulars sat in their regular seats, eating their regular food, drinking their regular drinks and carried on the regular conversations that occur in a city diner. A not so regular customer, Max Roebuck, sat on the end stool at the counter finishing a meat loaf plate.

Boss, the bald, heavy set, middle aged owner, was taking his afternoon break in front of the grill before the last evening spurt of customers converged. As usual during the break, he read aloud to his cronies from *The Boston Herald*. "Red Sox owner Jack Davidson stated "even though the event is purely charitable, Lugo is convinced his boys are going to give the Sox a run for their money." Boss looked up to reinforce the point. "You hear that? A run for their money."

As soon as he noticed his employees in their new jackets, he smiled and proudly boasted, "Here are our aces now. Our own Louisburg Sluggers. You guys ready for the big game?" All three, a bit embarrassed, smiled and nodded as they carefully hung up their jackets and put on their aprons.

One of the regulars, a surly sort who was rarely satisfied with anything in his own life, set his coffee mug down and sarcastically asked, "How do you guys find time to work with your busy schedule at Fenway?"

The question evoked laughter and banter among both the admiring and jealous patrons. One of the supporting regulars not liking the tone yelled loudly enough for the entire room to hear, "Hey. Why you bustin' their chops? Give 'em a break. They're just kids."

The support was lost on Frizz. He couldn't contain himself. "We may be kids, but we're gonna win."

The surly patron who had started it all laughed and became even more scornful. "Get a grip," he mocked. "We're talking the Boston Red Sox." He leaned toward Stretch with a look that said you dummy. "As in Major League."

Frizz had enough, especially considering his

earlier altercation. "We'll win. We got an edge."

Luther quickly grabbed Frizz's arm and whispered, "Shut up. We still don't want to get Hudson in trouble."

No one else overheard the remark. Except Max. It didn't take long for him to process it. Quick eyes and alert ears enabled him to drive his Mercedes, wear his Louis' suits and sport his gold Rolex. Max took a quick gulp of coffee, dropped a tenner on the counter and rushed out the door before the boys even noticed he was there.

Knowing the city like he did Max was able to negotiate the streets of the South End and make his B. I Lep way around The Public Garden to the foot of The Hill before Harmon parted ways with Roger and Cecil at the Beacon Hill subway stop. He was lucky enough to find an empty parking space at the station end of Charles Street. The crafty scout carefully tailed the teen carrying the mysterious black gym bag to his home on Louisburg Square.

When Harmon stepped into the study his father was already there. Professor Hudson, a grownup version of his son, looked up from his notes and glanced at the empty crate. "I thought I told you not to bother the helmet anymore. This is top secret." His tone became progressively sterner. "No more tampering. Understand?"

Fearing his whole plan might explode, Harmon's speech nervously sped up as he pleaded, "But Dad, it works. I've been using it for weeks. We got the game tomorrow and I made detailed records. Just like you taught me." He reached into the bag and laid his carefully penned account on the desk. In an attempt to reinforce his position, he added, "All these are backed up on the computer."

As Harmon watched, his still stern father began carefully examining the records. Harmon's voice became even more dire. "We can't stop now. I can't let the guys down and..." He paused thinking on his feet, "And all you need is empirical proof. The game tomorrow is the perfect place for that proof. Please, Dad. You gotta trust me."

Professor Hudson looked up from the records, which *were* complete and accurate, and into his son's searching eyes. The facts combined with Harmon's honest plea left him no choice. He conceded. "Okay. Just one more time. But I'm going to the game."

The father and son nodded and smiled at one another with warmth and mutual respect. They were so engrossed in the moment that neither noticed the well dressed scout who had seen and overheard everything from the open window.

102

With one problem out of the way an invigorated Harmon hustled to meet Roger and Cecil who had gone to the Esplanade hoping to encounter the girls. His friends however didn't share his newly found enthusiasm. The pensive duo sat on a bench not saying a word as the smiling Harmon stepped between them and their river view.

"What are you smiling about?" asked Cecil.

"Everything's cool with my dad. He's even coming to the game tomorrow."

Roger's head dropped. "What game? You heard Coach. We're not a team," he said without a ray of hope in his voice. Then he looked up and sighted the three beauties causing his whole demeanor to beam.

The standard awkward teen greetings were exchanged when the Latino girl had the where-with-all to ask, "Aren't you practicing for the game?"

Roger smiled, "You heard? The big game's tomorrow."

The tall one, Roger's favorite, shyly said, "Everybody's heard." This brought a boost in confidence and a real pride to the males who seem to gain height from the statement.

"Are you coming to the game?" Cecil asked.

All three girls answered in unison, "For sure," which caused laughter among the entire group.

The tall one coyly looked at Roger and walked away followed by her friends.

"See you tomorrow." She looked around and smiled.

"You got it," said Roger as the three watched the three walk away.

Changing the entire tone, Cecil asked, "So what are we going to do about tomorrow?"

Still watching the girls, Roger responded, "We're going to play as a team. I'm not going to blow my chance with them."

"We have to do it," Harmon said. "My dad's depending on me."

"We'll just do what has to be done," Cecil added. "No matter what."

Max Roebuck and Jack Davidson were already seated for an early dinner at Morton's Steak House. Davidson was sitting at his favorite table, drinking his favorite bourbon, waiting for his favorite strip cut when out of the corner of his eye he caught the first glimpse of a woman in her perfectly form fitting little black dress. She walked past the table giving a glance of recognition to Max who smiled and nodded.

Davidson commented, "Now that's a woman."

"She's Nate Lugo's daughter," said Max. He

watched Jo's every move as she walked across the room and sat at a table with three friends.

"She'll wish she were someone else's daughter after tomorrow's game." Davidson smugly lifted his bourbon glass as if to toast his remark, but instead said, "To their helmet and our wall."

Still looking toward Jo's table, a now unsmiling Max Roebuck clinked his glass against his boss'.

Priscilla Courtney had just finished moving into her new condo and was scanning the window of Yesterday's News as her Bichon Frise Missy sniffed the sidewalk and walls for dog evidence. Priscilla was surprised when she looked up to discover Nate Lugo bent down locking the door to his shop. When Nate straightened and recognized the window shopper, his face lit up.

"How are you, Mr. Lugo?"

"Fine, but I'd be better if you called me Nate."

"Then call me Priscilla. Fair enough?"

Both smiled and nodded.

"This is your antique shop, Nate?" Priscilla asked.

"Mine and my partner's," Nate said before redirecting the conversation. "I haven't seen you around here before."

"I'm not spying," said Priscilla with a hint of concern in her voice.

"A pretty lady like you doesn't need to spy."

Both smiled nervously.

"I just moved three blocks up The Hill into a condo on Joy Street. We're neighbors."

Nate looked down at Gunner who was acquainting himself with Missy in a very dog-like manner. "These two get along well," Priscilla commented.

"That's good," Nate said.

"Yes, it is."

Then the proverbial pregnant pause occurred as so often happens during first conversations when both parties care. Priscilla broke the silence, "So what are you doing the night before the big game?"

"Trying to keep it together, and it ain't easy right now." Nate expectantly looked into Priscilla's eyes. "You're coming to the game I hope."

"I wouldn't miss it for the world."

Nate smiled once again showing his delight. "Would you like to go for a cup of coffee?"

"That would be nice. I'd like that."

The happy four started down Charles Street to the corner coffee shop as the shadows cast on Beacon Hill became progressively fainter.

Twilight at the South End High ballfield looked quite different than twilight on Beacon Hill. A dirty, sweaty D.A. stood on the mound surrounded by practice balls. He hurled three perfect strikes to Luther who laid down three perfect bunts. As the third bunt came to a stop directly between home and first, Luther stuck out his chest and lip and mockingly boasted, "How good am I?"

D.A. smiled. "You sound like Sir Harmon Hudson."

A scoffing Luther punctuated the statement with, "That rich dink," causing D.A. to chuckle.

As D.A. started toward homeplate, Luther picked up his new glove and started toward the mound to complete the final switch of the evening. D.A. stopped him midway. "Coach says we're not a team, and he's right. You gotta talk to everybody."

"No way," Luther insisted. "They won't listen to me. They'll listen to you."

Not saying a word, the two stared into one another's face communicating as only very close friends can.

"That settles it," said Luther. "You're up."

D.A. walked to the plate to take his stance. Before he could set himself, he saw the pitch coming and still managed to slam a hard grounder. This time as Luther wound up, D.A. feigned a bunt causing both of them to crack up. Then D.A.

stepped back, went through his ritual and faced the mound. Luther threw a strike and with a smooth singular powerful motion, Richie D'Angelo sent the ball so high into the darkening sky it seemed to be chasing the sun.

~18~

The Independence Day sky was bright above Fenway but white and grey clouds alike appeared as if they were being gently and gradually shoved between the sun and the park. The Sox were on the field just finishing their warm up exercises and batting practice when Nat Lugo walked across his old familiar turf for the first time in years to shake hands with the opposing manager, Elliot Dryden, who was talking with the plate umpire. A few fans, mostly friends and families of both teams, were soaking in the summer rays or milling about enjoying the atmosphere of an old fashioned Fourth of July afternoon game.

Clyde Gooding and Billy Ray Block panned the scene then smiled at one another as they began setting up for their special WBZ-AM broadcast. Billy put on his headphones and adjusted the notes on his clipboard as Clyde tipped back his Optimo and, for the first time in a decade, flipped the switch on his microphone.

"Hello everybody. Clyde Gooding your fast ball announcer, bidding you a Happy Independence Day from Fenway Park in the heart of Boston where in just one hour the Sox and the Louisburg Sluggers will be taking to the field to benefit the Jimmy Fund."

As he had done thousands of times before, Billy Ray knew exactly when to cut in on his broadcast partner, "Yes indeed, ladies and gentlemen, we're here broadcasting from the nation's oldest ballpark. I'm Billy Ray Block, your screwball commentator) coming out of retirement with my old friend and colleague to bring you what promises to be an interesting afternoon of baseball."

The familiar sound of the announcers' voices brought smiles to the older fans' faces as they suddenly recovered a part of their sometimes forgotten childhoods. Even Clyde's enthusiasm began to grow as he looked over at his old friend and worked to get into the pace and rhythm of the banter. "We're in for a big treat today. In just one hour, our own Boston Red Sox will be taking the field against a group of very talented boys from neighborhoods throughout the city. Boston fans can't lose today as two hometown teams face off."

Then Billy Ray added, "It's cloudy, even threatening rain here, but hopefully it will hold off and the sun will shine for the Louisburg Sluggers in their major league debut. Great bunch of kids, huh Clyde?"

"You know it," Clyde said. "And I'm certain you'll enjoy the game and our pre-game show that includes interviews with members of both teams."

The mood in the Louisburg Sluggers locker room wasn't nearly as cheerful. The boys were much quieter than usual as Cecil lifted the helmet off Harmon. Now that all ten players had been programmed, Harmon carefully placed the device back into the black bag and sat down between Cecil and Roger. The rest of the group sat quietly on two other benches adjusting to their new game uniforms.

Luther elbowed D.A. and gave him a subtle reverse nod. D.A. stood and closed the door blocking the team from leaving, but also blocking the unseen Jo Lugo from coming in. Jo leaned her ear against the outside of the door as D.A. turned and faced the other nine boys.

"Before Miss Lugo gets back, I want everybody to listen up." D.A. assumed an extremely authoritative tone. "I got something to say." All the boys faced D.A. giving him their full attention. "The coach's whole life is riding on this game and he's depending on us. We ain't really a team. But today we're gonna be." He paused and looked down, then with an even more determined look, he stared at his team mates. "If anybody isn't willing, you can leave. But you gotta get through me." He paused again and once more panned all of their faces. "Anybody wanna leave?"

Silence consumed the room. All the Sluggers remained perfectly still. Except Harmon Hudson. Harmon walked up to D.A., gave a quick affirmative nod and extended his hand. As the two shook hands, Luther Gordon stepped up and put his hand over theirs. The other seven stood and followed his lead forming a circle of hands.

Roger Gray was the only one to say anything, a simple pronouncement, "Let's do it."

On the other side of the door, an elated Jo Lugo clinched both her fists and triumphantly punched the air while uttering under her breath, "Yes. Yes. Yes." She regained her game face, quickly knocked and walked into the locker room. "Okay, team," she said, this time meaning it. "It's time to take the field. Are you ready to go?"

"Let's go, Miss," said Facie.

The entire squad leapt out of the locker room like a big organism with a singular purpose. All of them came alive and were chattering with nervous excitement when they ran down the corridor and onto the perfectly manicured field. As the summer breeze hit their faces and the sound of the organ struck their ears, each of the boys had the feeling of being perfectly there, but not really there, as if in a dream. ~~they were in a dream~~

As soon as they hit the turf, the crowd went wild. They clapped, whistled, yelled, all standing as the Louisburg Sluggers floated over the green, brown and white field still feeling the strange sensation of bodily absence.

Clyde Gooding's voice rose above the sounds of the organ, "The fans love these boys, Billy Ray. What a response."

"You're right, Clyde. Today's crowd may be short on number, but they're certainly long on enthusiasm."

Gunner joined the boys and lumbered among them as they started their warmups, pepper games and stretching exercises. "All of them seem to like the Slugger's mascot," remarked Clyde. "He sure doesn't seem shy." Gunner's presence and the activity helped to eliminate some of the awe, but the nervous, serious looks on the boys' faces indicated it would take the concentration of the game to pull them down to earth.

Only Roger was all grins as he waved at D.A. and nodded to draw the latter's attention to the girls in the stands. Roger smiled and waved producing

an enthusiastic response in all the girls who in turn
waved back, laughed and commented to one
another about the cute players.

Billy Ray laughed at Clyde's remark as he
fixed his eyes on Gunner. "That's Nate Lugo's dog,
Gunner. For you radio listeners, he's a big bulldog.
Rumors tell he drinks Budweiser and eats Fenway
Franks."

The comment caused Clyde to laugh as well.
"Sounds like a typical Boston weight watcher, Billy."

Down on the field Nate Lugo stood pensively
as his team positioned themselves for batting
practice. Jo walked up to her concerned father and
put her arm around him. "Everything's going to be
all right, Dad. You've got yourself a team."

"You sure?"

"I'm sure," she said patting his shoulder. "I
know character when I see it."

~19~

Waking dreams are much different than sleeping dreams. And so it was for the Louisburg Sluggers until their ideal world was broken by a comment of a jealous bat boy as the Red Sox made their way to the locker room. "These guys must be lost," the intruder purposely uttered at high volume. "The Little League field's in Brighton."

All of the Sluggers and some of the Sox heard the comment. A few of the pros chuckled, but their catcher Jason Basavich didn't. He promptly chided the bat boy, "Hey. You're outta line."

Hating that anyone should step on his hard earned moments, Roger immediately went for the smart aleck. "We're gonna kick your butts."

D.A. grabbed Roger's elbow and assuredly whispered, "We'll show 'em."

While all this was going on, Jo was catching

Harmon's warm up pitches. Even though she had been an All American softball player in college, she was barely able to handle the steam. At one point after catching a curve, she looked up and locked eyes with Max Roebuck. Her smile was involuntary. So was Max's. The old flame that had been burning a lot of years was still as hot as one of Harmon's fastballs.

A spectator sitting behind Max mistook the direction of the smile. He turned to Professor Hudson seated next to him and asked, "Is that lady smiling at you or me?"

Hudson leaned back as proud fathers are often prone to do and answered the question indirectly, "That's my son pitching to her. She's his coach."

Hearing this, Max turned and recognized the professor he had spied on the night before and then turned his attention back to the field. Each of the Sluggers took a few minutes hitting. The crack of the bats interspersed with the crack of the ball hitting Jo's mitt was something to hear. The rhythmic popping was so loud it cut all the way to the announcer's booth causing Billy Ray to cover his mic. He motioned for Clyde to do the same. "What the hell is going on down there?" he asked.

Clyde could merely respond by shaking his head from side to side. "I can't tell the crack of the bat from the crack of the ball hitting the mitt."

Billy Ray's decades of observation and ongoing curiosity began to fuse. "I've seen those swings before." He looked to his old friend, and in order to reinforce his position, repeated, "I know I've seen those swings before."

Clyde nodded in agreement and for the first time began to realize what Nate Lugo meant when he told them they had waited all their lives for this. He smiled at the cleverness of the old line batting coach as he uncovered and shared his new found expectation with the crowd. The sound of Clyde Gooding's voice filled the park going inside the heads of each of the fans. "I have a feeling this is going to be a special day for The Game."

The phenomena did not go unnoticed on the field either. The Sox equipment manager Howie Dingle had been intently watching the batting practice. In years of preparing the gear and then having to sit for long periods before he was needed again, Howie like Max had honed his watching and listening skills to the point that few things in his immediate environment escaped him. When he saw the two veterans in the booth talking between themselves and heard the last crack from the last batter, he rushed off the field and to the locker room as if he were the Paul Revere of baseball.

By the time he reached the dressing room, he

was barely able to contain himself. His speech was loud and fast. "Elliot! You gotta see these kids! They're good! I mean really good!"

This evoked laughter from the managers, coaches and players alike who were still in their charitable, holiday mode.

"Yeah, Howie," mocked Elliot, "We'll probably run through our whole pitching staff today." He turned to address the entire room in a serious manner to put everything back into perspective. "Look. This is for the Jimmy Fund. Besides that, it'll mean the world to these kids and the rest of the kids around the city. Have some fun out there. After all, it is a kids' game." He slapped his hands together to emphasize that the Sox should give them and all the fans the best show they could. "Okay guys, let's hit it." Then giving Howie an obvious sidelong glance, Elliot could not resist one last barb, "If you're not too nervous."

A laughing, confident Red Sox team took the field leaving Howie Dingle standing alone in the locker room.

~20~

When the Louisburg Sluggers, bats in hands, took their position along the first base line awaiting the national anthem, the feeling of being there but not being there returned to all of them as they looked at their heroes standing along the third base line. From a birds eye view, the vee formed by the two teams certainly looked lopsided as the much bigger Sox stood their ground.

But lopsided was the way that Jack Davidson liked it, especially when the weight leaned in his favor. He watched the proceedings on the huge screen in his office as Clyde's sober, familiar request rang over the public address, "Ladies and gentlemen, please stand for our national anthem."

When the words *Oh say, can you see* came through the speakers, Davidson smiled inside as he said to himself, "Oh yeah. I can see it all. And it looks good from here."

Still in thought, he swiveled his chair toward his henchman, a dark sinister looking character in black sunglasses with a scorpion tattooed on the side of his neck just below his right ear. He was aptly nicknamed Creeps.

Davidson confided to Creeps, "Roebuck has assured me that he'll blow the cover on this technical charade and we'll come out on top even if we lose the game." The last three words that came out of his mouth seemed to sour as they took form and caused Davidson to lift his left nostril in a sneer. "I don't like that attitude. I didn't get to where I am today by losing."

Creeps sat motionless as a sponge heeding every word and watching every move, soaking up the situation and the instructions. Davidson rose and walked in front of Creeps placing his outstretched hands on the arms of his henchman's chair. He leaned into his loyal employee's face and staring at his own reflection in the sunglasses emphasized the orders, "When you hear from me, I want Lugo out of the game. Lugo loves that dog. Take the dog out and Lugo is out. Understand?"

Davidson began nodding his head up and down causing Creeps to mimic the motion. The two were in complete agreement.

Now that Davidson's insurance was in place a knowing smile adorned his face. The determined, focused Creeps made his way out of the office and on to Fenway Park as the words *the land of the free and the home of the brave* wafted through the speakers.

"Creeps" - enforce

~21~

*last two words
of NA at a ball
game*

All diehard baseball fans know the last two
words of our national anthem, and in this
game as in every major league game, they
came from the man behind the plate. "Play ball,"
the umpire screamed.

Both the fans in the park and those listening
to their radios could hear the joy and excitement in
Clyde Gooding's voice as he watched the Louisburg
Sluggers take the field and announced the first
words of the game, "As an act of good will, the Sox
gave the local boys the choice to field or bat first and
it looks like the Sluggers took the home team option.
We also want to take this opportunity to thank WBZ
radio and the Boston Red Sox for co-sponsoring this
special hometown holiday broadcast."

An equally enthusiastic Billy Ray Block
chimed in, "The Sox are all around generous hosts

today, Clyde. Each of the players is giving the Jimmy Fund a thousand dollars out of his own pocket to be donated along with the front office's contribution."

"I understand that's quite a sum, Billy."

"You bet it is. If the Sox win, it's $25,000, but should the Louisburg Sluggers take the game, it'll be a cool million to the Jimmy Fund."

Clyde responded, "That's a long shot, but the gesture is sure generous."

As the two continued to talk, Nate Lugo walked out to Harmon and handed him the game ball. The computer expert looked a bit out of place and a lot out of sorts.

Nate winked. "You're okay, kid. Once you throw that first pitch, all those butterflies will flutter off and out of the stadium." He gave Harmon an encouraging slap on the arm, turned and went to take his place in the dugout.

On the walk back Nate looked into the stands to notice Priscilla holding Missy. She smiled, blew Nate a kiss and mouthed, "Good luck."

Nate returned the smile and in a gentlemanly fashion doffed his cap as he stepped down into the dugout where Gunner was waiting and watching. He directed a question to his little friend. "What do you think of those two ladies, Gunner?"

As if he understood, Gunner answered with a

underhand
push

bark causing Nate to smile even more, But the look
on Nate's face immediately became serious as he
turned his attention to the game and watched the
Sox lead off hitter come to the plate.

Clyde's voice filled the park, "Leading off for
the Red Sox is center fielder, Johnny Daley."

Harmon watched as the much bigger Daley
took his stance, stared the kid straight in the eye,
smiled and spit toward the mound. But a dropped
jaw quickly altered the smile when Harmon blasted
his first pitch past Daley. Clyde's voice rang
through the speakers. "Strike one. A very fast
fastball there, Billy Ray."

Even though Daley was set for the second
pitch, he wasn't ready for the speed. Again he heard
the speaker. "Another one down the center for a call
strike two."

The Sox management came off the bench
when beckoned by the operator who was astounded
at the 1-0-4 registering on his speed clock. The
second pitch brought the entire Sox team off the
bench. Billy Ray's voice seemed gleeful as he
commented, "Was that fast ball fast or what? I think
that speed clock must be broken."

Johnny Daley was even more confused as he
swung as hard and fast as he could to no avail. This
time he heard the ump yell strike three and was
more than addled as he shook his head and started

back to the dugout. En route he met Elliot Dryden loudly complaining to the umpire about Harmon's motion. As soon as Daley reached the dugout, the Sox were all over him.

"I didn't know where the ball was going," Daley said. "I couldn't handle the motion."

From the announcers' booth, Billy Ray mused. "There seems to be some commotion from the Sox dugout, Clyde. Manager Elliot Dryden seems a bit upset with the situation."

"The umpire is motioning both Dryden and Lugo to the mound," Clyde said.

Elliot and Nate gathered around the rubber with the umpire while Harmon stood awaiting instructions. An extremely upset Elliot was the first to speak. "The pitcher's motion is illegal."

Nate almost laughed at Elliot's reaction. "The only infraction you can get him for is speeding, Elliot. What the hell are you complaining about?"

"It's illegal according to Major League rules," retorted Elliot.

Nate remained calm. "It may not be typical, but I can clear this up." Nate whistled loudly and motioned to both Cecil and Priscilla to come to the mound.

When Priscilla arrived, the umpire half apologetically said, "I usually make these calls, Ma'am, but this game is unusual."

"What's the problem?" Priscilla asked.

Elliot answered, "Illegal pitching motion. Major League rules."

Before Priscilla could respond, Cecil stepped in, "Sir, I know you're aware it wasn't until 1884 that pitchers threw overhand.

"So what?" said Elliot.

"Unusual, yes. But not illegal," responded Cecil.

Elliot frowned down at Cecil as if to say *who in the hell are you,* but instead of speaking, he looked to Priscilla for support.

"The kid's right, Elliot," she said.

As the others left the mound, Harmon turned to Frizz Stephens, smiled and winked which caused Frizz to beam and chatter his support. "Rock and Fire, Harmon. Rock and Fire."

"Some question about motion," Billy Ray reported, "but everything seems settled and it's time to play ball."

~22~

At that moment Harmon Hudson had it all going for him. His teammates supported, even liked him, his coach had complete confidence in him and the umpires sanctioned his motion. With all that under his belt, he summarily fanned Collazo and Rivera then started to the dugout all smiles. Even Clyde and Billy Ray whose years of announcing experience had polished their ability to dramatize seemed understated in their shared reportage.

Clyde shook his head in disbelief. "That's three up and three down for the Sox who have yet to get wood on the ball."

Billy Ray immediately chimed in, "The Sox seemed stunned by these kids."

The players weren't the only ones stunned. As they took the field waiting for the Sluggers to bat,

Elliot Dryden frowned and sheepishly looked at Howie Dingle. "This is serious," he said removing his cap and running his hand through his thinning hair. "Who is this kid?"

Howie, who only minutes earlier, was the butt of a great joke now spoke with the confidence of one vindicated. "I hate to say I told you so, Chief, but you ain't seen nothin' yet."

"Shut up, Howie." Elliot jerked the cap back onto his head. "I have to think. Three batters, three outs. We got a problem here."

An even bigger problem came for the manager when the dugout phone rang. Howie quickly picked it up, but was even quicker to hand it to Elliot when he heard the irate voice on the other end. As usual Jack Davidson was very blunt. "What just happened?"

"How should I know? You saw it the same as me."

"Fix it now." Davidson slammed down the phone.

Elliot handed the receiver back to Howie and once again turned his complete attention to the game just as Cecil stepped into the batter's box. Cecil felt a jolt of nervous pride as he heard Clyde's voice say his name over the loud speakers for the first time. "Leading off for the Louisburg Sluggers is the catcher, Cecil Underwood, facing Owen Reid on the mound for the Sox."

All the words that followed were lost on him as his intense concentration turned solely to the ball. "The wind up. The delivery," Clyde said in anticipation of the first Sox pitch of the game.

As Cecil *ala* Pete Rose watched the ball leave Reid's hand, he instinctively knew a fastball was coming. An unblinking eye followed the ball and a series of muscles from the toes through the legs into the torso onto the shoulders down the arms and ending in the thumbs and fingers in perfect sequence and coordination placed all of their power into the ball through the sweet spot of the bat as the nine-inch sphere shot out of the infield into right center where Johnny Daley with equal perfection fielded the blast. But not in time to prevent Cecil from pulling into second with a standup double.

Unlike the screaming, smiling fans going wild over their hometown teens, Elliot Dryden was screaming but not smiling. "They hit too?" he barked at his equipment manager. Howie merely shrugged prompting, "Great. Just great," from Elliot.

The whole of Fenway Park became a hive of excitement mixed with incredulity as Roger Gray singled to right field sending Cecil to third. The mere fact that two kids got clean hits off a major league hurler upset all expectations. Even the fans who had gone for refreshments were drawn back to the field as Luther Gordon loosened up and stepped into the batter's box.

Jo Lugo smiled at Luther and winked as she watched her player-student boldly take his stance and face off with a confidence far beyond his years. After taking the first two pitches, Luther stepped into a low fast ball sending it deep into the right field corner. Jo gasped along with the rest of the crowd when Luther was robbed of a home run with an impressive stretch-catch by the Sox right fielder. Luther was all smiles as he returned to the dugout along with Cecil and his first major league RBI. His excitement even blocked out Clyde's comment about the Sluggers scoring before the Sox.

Nate clapped his hands, gave D.A. a hit away nod and signaled to Roger who carefully took a long lead. On the second pitch, Roger bolted as D.A. pounded a slider sending a shot directly to the center field wall. The spin of the ball caused a skewed carom onto the grass. Nate's arms circled in excitement as he motioned Roger around third and into home for the second run of the game by the unlikely underdogs. Clyde's voice pealed over the loud, now standing crowd. "Who'da thunk it? That's the second run for our local boys here in the bottom of the first."

Once again Nate signaled for a hit away.

Frizz Stephens responded with a blast to left sending D.A. home from his perch on second. With little attention in his direction, Frizz's attempt to stretch his clean single to a double resulted in the second out and prompted a comment from Billy Ray. "The kid's fast, Clyde, but not that fast."

When Harold Chavez grounded out to short, the now relieved Sox returned to their dugout still stunned by the action. A lot of heads were shaking after looking at the scoreboard that read 0-3 at the bottom of the first. The crowd buzzed with excitement wondering what was coming next.

"These kids are really looking good," was Billy Ray's final comment before covering his mic and signaling Clyde to do the same. "Did you see that swing?" he asked.

"Short on the bat and quick," Clyde said, well knowing each had seen it before, but not quite able to pinpoint where.

In the Sox dugout, the phone pulsed out an angry ring. Again Howie picked it up and again he immediately handed it to Elliot.

"What the hell is going on?" said an even more irate Jack Davidson.

"I don't know," answered Elliot. "I'm trying to figure it out."

Davidson quieted down, but Elliot knew the softer comment was much stronger. "You better figure it out," he said. "You embarrass me and I'll bury you."

~23~

When the Red Sox came to bat in the second, the park had quieted down. The buzz had become a calm, intense focus as players and fans alike scrutinized the small bespeckled figure on the mound. The near silence was broken by Clyde Gooding's voice. "That brings up the Sox designated hitter David Mendez to lead off here in the second."

Mendez was well familiar with the pressure of expectation placed on a player whose sole purpose was to hit. But even being the best in the league at his craft did not prepare him for what was to come in the next few seconds. For the first time in years David Mendez swung far behind a fastball. It was clocked at 1-1-1. The second pitch was a much slower curve ball, the break of which Mendez had never seen. The addled but cool professional simply stepped back from the plate and ran his hand up the bat in an attempt to regain his composure.

On the other hand, Clyde Gooding nearly came off his seat. "Did you see that curveball?" he chuckled as he queried. The volume of his voice increased. "The only place the ball is bouncing is back into Hudson's glove. The Sox are still trying to get a handle on his motion."

Elliot Dryden did come off his seat in the Sox dugout, called time and walked over to David Mendez.

"How do you read it?" he asked Mendez.

"Fastball's like lightning." He turned his palms upward. "That curve broke a good foot and a half."

Elliot put his arms behind his back, hooked his fingers over his belt and stared at the ground. After a few seconds of thought, he reached the only logical conclusion. He looked at his prime hitter and plainly instructed, "Come around as fast as you can. If you get wood on it, the ball will give you the power. Hit away."

Mendez nodded his understanding, walked beside the batter's box and grabbed dirt as Elliot returned to the dugout. The timeout had allowed him to totally regain his composure and with renewed determination, he stepped up to the plate. His eyes followed the ball as it left Harmon's hand except unlike the previous two failures, he used all of his experience and expertise and led the blurring sphere like a hunter leads a swift quail. His severe concentration paid off with the crack of wood crossing horsehide. The ball lined deep into right center and a smiling David Mendez pulled into second.

The Red Sox bench came alive. Players and managers alike were on their feet cheering and waving and whistling to their designated hitter.

"Wow, did that ever electrify the Sox bench," Clyde commented. "Mendez has opened the door for Don Krevitz to see if the first sacker can come through with a hit."

Krevitz hit the ball to first for a fielder's choice advancing Mendez to third. The Sox had begun to connect using Elliot's method. Jason Basavich, the Sox catcher stepped up and swung with the power that had enabled him to chalk up fifteen homeruns that season. His strike was so strong that it caused Billy Ray to comment, "What a swing by Basavich, Clyde. I felt the breeze way up here."

Basavich calmly stepped back into the box. His lightning swing on the second pitch connected sending the ball deep into center field scoring Mendez. "Whew. He sure came around quick enough to tag that one," Clyde said.

Billy Ray laughed. "Lucky it wasn't a curve."

After stealing second on a bobbled pitch, Basavich was driven in by Curt Carter, the right fielder. Sox second baseman, Mark Briscoe grounded out to short to end the inning but not before the Boston Red Sox put two runs on the scoreboard.

"Now we have a ballgame, Clyde," Billy Ray commented. "This is definitely a hitters' day."

~24~

Billy Ray Block had no idea of the understatement of his comment. The strong hitting Sox had gotten a handle on Harmon's motion and were able to play like they had never played. Not only was their hitting at its best, the fielding exhibition showed the small crowd why they earned the honor of being called *Major League*.

By the end of the third the scoreboard read Sox-7, Sluggers-8. And Billy Ray showed Clyde his Louisburg Slugger lineup with five hitters from the past whose swings the apt detective had identified. The slugfest continued and by the bottom of the fifth, the scoreboard read Sox-14, Sluggers-15.

Clyde and Billy Ray now knew that Nate Lugo was not kidding. After all, he never kidded about baseball. But this exceeded all expectations and the waves that emanated from the Fenway Park sound booth across Boston on that Independence Day carried with them the excitement of the two veteran announcers who thought they had seen it all.

"What a day," Clyde said. "What a game. In fact, it's the game of games, the show of shows. The only thing missing is a full stadium. If you love baseball, you've got to come to Fenway. Plenty of seats for all. I have a feeling we're about to witness baseball history."

With equal enthusiasm Billy Ray joined in. "Clyde's right, fans. Drop whatever you're doing. Park your cars, leave your yard work, forget your barbeques and bring your kids to the park. The best fireworks in New England are here at Fenway." Then with even greater enthusiasm he added, "Baseball is back."

Even Davidson's threatening calls couldn't squelch the excitement in the Sox dugout. This time when the phone rang, Howie, not saying a word, merely tilted his head to the side and with a ho-hum look handed the receiver to Elliot. All Elliot heard was Jack Davidson yelling, "You're dead meat, Dryden. I..." and that's all it took for the manager to drop the handset into the water bucket.

He turned to smile at his gape-mouthed equipment manager and offered a simple explanation. "Wrong number," he said before turning his entire focus back to the game.

In the other dugout, Jo Lugo was equally focused except for a moment between innings when she looked into the stands to see Max Roebuck standing behind the Sluggers. Max smiled and looked down sheepishly leaving Jo somewhat perplexed, but when Harold Chavez asked her a quick question, she immediately redirected her attention.

Both teams continued to pelt the ball and cross the plate causing both scores to steadily climb. They were further encouraged by the increasing energy of the excited fans who had never witnessed such a demonstration. The cheering became louder and louder and the available seats became fewer and fewer.

Everyone in the park was concentrating on the figures on the field as well as the figures on the scoreboard which rose to an astounding 25 to 23 Sox favor by the bottom of the eighth. So no one in the park noticed an arm wearing a gold Rolex remove the black bag situated in a corner of the Louisburg Slugger's dugout. *may*

~25~

A light, drizzle lingered as the Louisburg Sluggers scored again with a series of three singles to shrink the Sox lead to one run. As the lead shrank, the crowd grew until most of the seats filled. Just outside the park, instead of the usual trickle of cars on a lazy Fourth of July afternoon, a gush of traffic turned Kenmore Square into an eight block parking lot.

In the midst of the mania, the plate umpire stepped onto the field to stop the game. But not because of rain. He called Elliot Dryden out of the dugout who in turn called out Howie Dingle who rushed to the Sox locker room for of all things, more baseballs.

When Billy Ray figured out what was going on he smiled and leaned into the mic. "I've never seen this before. The plate umpire sent the Sox equipment manager to get more baseballs. Clyde, can you believe it? They've run out of baseballs."

"Everything about this day is different," Clyde said. "Now we're getting reports of a thunderstorm with flash flood warnings working its way towards the park. You fans sit tight so you don't lose your seats. I've been assured this will blow over in a matter of minutes." As they were speaking, dark ominous clouds moved over and around the park. Along with the descending darkness came the third Slugger out.

A detail cop who had worked his way through traffic and parked his cruiser behind the Green Monster switched to the AM dial just in time to hear Clyde give the update on the game that was now the talk of the town. "That's the third out for the Louisburg Sluggers here in the bottom of the eighth making the score Sox, 25-Sluggers, 24. And none too early as the ump just called in the ground crew to pull the tarp over the infield."

A few blocks away at the Elizabeth Diner, Boss leaned back on his stool and with an open palm slapped the counter causing the large group of regulars congregated around the radio to jump.

"This game ought to be on T.V." he exclaimed. "Those kids deserve it."

Not one of the patrons disagreed, not even the Doubting Thomas who only a few hours before had taken pleasure in the goading. As so often happens with those who distinguish themselves as extraordinary, the three busboys became the property of a group who proudly and affectionately claimed ownership.

As Clyde and Billy Ray awaited their ON AIR light following the commercials, Billy Ray slid his Louisburg Slugger roster along with eight of the corresponding greats in front of his partner. Clyde appreciatively nodded his approval and smiled just as the red light flashed to indicate they were on air.

"Welcome back to Fenway, listeners. The tarp is still on the field but you wouldn't know it by the behavior of the fans. They're pouring into the park faster than the rain. We've just gone from full capacity to standing room only."

The area around the cruiser behind the left field wall was as packed as the park, but the detail cop didn't mind. He smiled as the crowd around the blue and white car strained to hear when the game of games would resume.

A mere two blocks away in Kenmore Square, Max Roebuck, ill-gotten gain in hand, meandered through the foot traffic under the CITGO sign. "I got the bag," he reported to Jack Davidson on his mobile phone. "If you think the traffic's bad, you should try walking through this crowd."

A sharp "Get it up here now," was Davidson's only reply.

As Davidson's spoke, an equally sharp bolt of lightning along with its deafening thunder shot through the Boston sky and smashed just below the large triangle sign causing a collective gasp in the entire Fenway area.

~26~

The scare was immediate and temporary. Except for Max Roebuck who found himself stranded against the wall of the building that supported the familiar landmark. The bolt had not harmed the Citgo sign but it had torn away its main power cable which had dropped and was now swinging back and forth like a huge serpent holding Max hostage on an island of concrete. As the heavy cable erratically arced, it hit the puddles on either side of him and created sparks with each contact.

A Boston cop surveyed the situation. He immediately noticed the devastating fear in Max's eyes and quickly gave the encouraging order, "Stay still, Buddy. The firemen are coming."

Just as he spoke, a fire truck pulled on the scene and the crew took immediate action. The chief barked his order before his boot hit the asphalt.

"We can't get a ladder in there because of the wire. Turn off the juice"

A veteran firemen used to such on the spot decisions immediately responded, "No time to find the box."

Both watched as the wire continued to swing erratically. "If the wind catches that wire the wrong way, he's fried," the chief said. "Let's form a hand to hand line to get him out of there."

"Who can lift him?" asked the veteran.

Before any of the crew could respond, a bystander yelled, "Popeye can."

The Chief cupped his hands and shouted at the running bystander, "Who's Popeye?"

"The sausage vendor. He can lift anything."

By the time the bystander and Popeye returned, the firemen were lined up and ready for action. Popeye indeed looked like he could lift the statehouse. The vendor's forearms were disproportionately huge. *like oak tree* *tree limbs*

The Chief gave him instructions as they walked to the head of the line. Popeye nodded understanding and took his position as the last link in a human chain comprised of him and the supporting firefighters and policemen. The two firemen directly behind him securely grasped his belt. Behind them, four more of the links grasped their belts and behind them the anchoring eight braced themselves for the rescue.

Popeye, whose eyes seemed as big as his forearms looked directly into Max's eyes. "Get rid of that baggage, Son," he softly instructed. Max briefly looked at the bag and flung it to the other side of the water.

Popeye watched carefully as the wire began syncopating. Max began moving with the cable's rhythm as both he and Popeye timed the swing. Each time it came near the water, sparks flew and Max instinctively backed up trying to imbed himself into the safety of the dry brick wall.

"When the cable reaches the end of its arc, lean over and grab my hand, Son," Popeye instructed. "Trust me. I won't let you fall."

Max looked into the big smiling eyes knowing if he were electrocuted, the entire group would suffer the same fate. But as the cable reached its apogee, he did trust and fell toward his rescuer. Max had never felt such a strong, consistent grip. With seeming effortlessness, Popeye lifted him up and across the water to safety. The group of onlookers immediately broke into cheers along with the cops and firefighters who were slapping Popeye on the back and congratulating one another.

As Max's fear turned to relief, he faced the entire group and offered a humble, "Thanks. Thanks to all of you." Then with a total lack of self consciousness, he hugged the vendor. "Especially you," he said.

Popeye smiled. "Looks like you could use a sausage," he said evoking laughter from the entire crowd.

The Chief handed Max the black bag. "You okay?" he asked. "That was a close call." Max smiled and nodded as his mobile phone rang. "You seem all right now," the Chief added. "You on your way to the game?"

"I'm on my way back," Max said as he shook the Chief's hand. The phone rang a third time. Max answered, "Yeah."

Jack Davidson was well on his way to complete frustration. "Where are you?" he shouted. Still a bit shaken, Max delayed his answer just long enough for Davidson to say, "Hold on."

Davidson laid down the desk phone to take the call on his mobile phone. Max could overhear Davidson's side of the conversation with Creeps. He knew by the owner's emphatic tone, which he'd often experienced, that his action was imperative. "Plan B right away," Davidson ordered. "I want Lugo out of the game. Get the damn dog. Now!"

By the time Davidson hung up, Max was running back to the park carrying the black bag.

"Roebuck," Davidson said alerting his need for immediate attention. When he heard nothing on the other end, his eyes shifted between both his phones. He knew Max was no longer his. Aloud and to himself he said, "He's gone back. The son of a ..."

~27~

Like the veteran firefighter, Jack Davidson was a man of quick decision and equally quick action. As soon as he hung up the phone, he called his security chief at Fenway Park. The civil behavior of the crowd had lulled the chief into thinking everything was going great guns, so the disruptive tone of his feared boss's voice caught him off guard.

"Jack Davidson here."

"Yes sir, Mr. Davidson," he answered not knowing what the next roar would bring.

Davidson vented as he ordered. "Max Roebuck's finished. He's coming into the park with a bag. It's mine. I want that bag. Got it?"

The security chief didn't understand why, but he did know who and what, so he subserviently replied, "Yes sir. Got it." As soon as the receiver hit the cradle, he was on the two-way sending out an all points bulletin to his entire force to stop Max Roebuck and get the bag.

Already inside the park, Max had anticipated the move putting him one step ahead of them. He evaded all the guards by weaving through the aisles among the shoulder to shoulder crowd until he came to the row where Professor Hudson was sitting. As he reached his destination, the ground crew had finished lifting the tarp and the sky turned clear and bright.

The only thing lighter than the day was Clyde's voice announcing, "For once the weather people were right. The rain has stopped as fast as it started and the umpire has given the go ahead."

Max wriggled his way across the feet and legs of the wet, grumpy spectators. He stopped just before reaching the professor's seat. Professor Hudson adopted a look that questioned Max's presence and intention. Knowing his time was limited, Max cut to the chase.

"You don't know me, but I'm a friend of Nate Lugo. I have something in this bag that belongs to you." Max saw the two guards entering the section before they could spot him. "Move over. I have to sit down," he pleaded.

The professor moved and Max squeezed in between him and a super-sized body builder. When the big guy moved his blue bag, Max noticed the name *VINCE* printed on a tag in large block letters.

"Hey, Vince," Max asked, "want to make a quick five hundred?"

"No problem as long as it's legal."

"What's in your bag?"

"Workout clothes. I just came from the gym."

Max pulled five one-hundred dollar bills from his wallet and extended them to Vince. "For the bag and clothes?" he asked.

"Oh yeah," said Vince grabbing the five hundred. "It's all yours buddy."

Max quickly emptied both bags. He carefully placed the helmet in the blue bag, rapidly stuffed the sweaty workout clothes, weight belt and sneakers in the black bag and handed the blue bag to the professor.

"You gotta get out of here," he said. "Go."

Professor Hudson wasted no time in leaving up the left aisle. Max shot up the right aisle carrying the black bag. Now he wanted to be seen. It took a matter of seconds before the two guards converged on him. "We're sorry, Mr. Roebuck," the shorter of the two said, "but we need that bag."

Without saying a word, Max elbowed his way through the crowd away from Professor Hudson's path. The guards continued the pursuit while alerting the other troops of Max's whereabouts. The clamor caused by the chase first drew attention in the immediate vicinity but soon spread downward until the entire section along with the players and coaches were distracted.

Jo Lugo shaded her eyes to investigate the commotion but instead of seeing Max, she spotted the sinister character with the scorpion tattoo she had seen on Charles Street. He was carrying a white drawstring bag that was violently wiggling. Instinctively, Jo turned to the dugout where Gunner had been patiently waiting for the rain to stop. She yelled and pointed at Creeps. "He's got Gunner. Dad, that man has Gunner."

Hearing the name of his beloved dog, Nate Lugo winced and jumped into the stands running like a man four decades younger.

In the meantime, Max had played harum-scarum with the guards long enough to ensure Professor Hudson's escape. When he was confident the professor was safely out of the clutches of Davidson's men, he allowed a group of a dozen to surround him. It was then he spotted Creeps running with the wriggling white bag. Knowing Davidson's plan, he dropped the black bag and quickly switched from prey to predator. Under orders to get only the bag, the guards parted quite satisfied their mission was accomplished.

Creeps' burden of a big squirming bulldog gave Max the upper hand. He picked up the pace chasing Creeps at top speed when Nate emerged from a side corridor and collided with his protege.

"He's got Gunner."

"I know, Nate. But we'll get him back."

Now running side by side, Max and Nate hounded Creeps and his precious ransom further down into the bowels of Fenway. But Nate Lugo knew Fenway Park. For years it was his territory. "Go towards the field so you can cut him off," he gasped and continued his direct path toward Creeps.

Max did as instructed.

The scene outside the park was much calmer. Making his way down Brookline Avenue, Professor Hudson with the blue bag strapped over his shoulder like a self-assured boy running away from home excitedly punched ten numbers into his mobile phone. On the other end, a phone in a quiet Virginia office rang. As always, the desk with the large C.I.A. seal above it was manned and ready to transfer any and all information at a moment's notice.

"Roberts here," sounded the unemotional voice.

"Hudson here," replied the professor. "It works. The report will be on your desk in three days."

When he heard the click on the other end, Theodore Hudson pocketed his phone and fled the final testing ground of his project.

~28~

ax had a clear view as he ran down the corridor parallel to Creeps and his burden. When he judged he was near or ahead of his target, he struck a sharp left through a connecting tunnel and came up six feet behind Creeps. Both men were tired and breathing hard, but Max knew he still had a lot left in him, so with one determined leap he easily made the tackle and took his adversary to the concrete.

Creeps dropped the bag. When it hit the floor, the unshaken bulldog wiggled his way out and shot through the nearest doorway to escape his unsavory captor who was already on his feet.

And Creeps would have recaptured him immediately if it weren't for the unrelenting effort of Max who grabbed the henchman's leg before he could start for Gunner. The move immediately put *nefarious*

Creeps on the offense. He turned and kicked Max in the stomach. Max let go, but Creeps had just begun. He repeatedly kicked Max in the ribs and then in the face leaving him down and hurt. Then he quickly resumed his nefarious mission.

By that time Gunner had made his way onto the weight activated dumbwaiter running up the side of the Green Monster. The small old-fashioned elevator which for decades had been used to hoist the thousands of gallons of green paint up the wall now had a much different cargo. The clever bulldog seemed a bit surprised by the upward movement, but was glad to be in his protective cubby as Creeps, trying to grasp him, missed his elusive mark. Creeps quickly evaluated his options and started up the ladder beside the dumbwaiter.

Gunner reached the top of the wall while Creeps was only three-fourths of the way there. This was clearly a situation in which four feet were superior to two. The bulldog easily negotiated his way across the narrow walkway of the wall and was at the far end overlooking left center when Creeps stepped off the ladder.

Gunner looked at his predator and sneezed as Creeps worked to gain his balance on the narrow path. Creeps stretched out his arms like a high wire walker and began his tightrope trek. Still standing at the far end and only briefly taking his eyes off his rival, Gunner sized up his situation. The jump was too high, but he was cornered, so he did what any self respecting male bulldog would do. He marked his territory. Walking back three feet, Gunner liberally urinated on the wall creating his own little private pond and then returned to his perch on the end. Creeps, still trying to maintain his balance, was totally unaware of the action, but he looked up when Gunner started barking at him.

A spectator in the bleachers also heard the bark. Then two spectators. Then three. Then an entire section became aware of the odd presence of the two creatures on the wall. But they were far more interested in the fate of the dog than the man. By the time everyone in the bleachers was watching, the pointing had stopped and the chanting began. "Jump. Jump. Jump. Jump. Jump. Jump," they intoned encouraging Gunner to make a leap of escape into the center-field bleachers. The chant became so loud that it reached the ears in the booth.

"The sun's out again and we're ready to resume the game, Billy Ray" reported Clyde. Hearing the chant he added, "The crowd is really excited."

His colleague responded, "Those of you in the radio audience are missing quite a show. The folks here at Fenway are being entertained by what *nemesis* *cadence*

seems to be a tightrope act on the Green Monster."

Handing Billy Ray the binoculars, Clyde added, "That's Nate Lugo's dog, but I don't recognize the fellow following him."

Nate had just stepped onto the field. Hearing the announcement, he looked to the top of the wall and his concern rapidly deepened. Not taking his eyes from his beloved pet, he powerlessly made his way across the grass.

Gunner's attention, on the other hand, was divided. Between turning to look down at the crowd and turning to judge the proximity of his nemesis, he barely had time to bark.

Then he saw it.

One of the "jump jump" chanters held his arm at full length keeping cadence with the crowd. In his right hand was of all things, a Fenway Frank, balanced only by a near full cup of Budweiser in his left hand. Gunner's eyes locked on the fan, then on the prize. The decision was clinched.

Any Broadway choreographer would pray for the inspiration of the movement in the following seven seconds. Gunner backed up, shifted his weight from feet to feet, licked his lips, quick-stepped to the edge and leapt toward his favorite meal.

In the meantime, Creeps, who had inched his way to within two yards of the edge, was surprised to see Gunner shorten the gap and turn his back. When he realized the dog's intentions, fear abandoned him and he lunged for his prey.

But the puddle prevented the capture. Creep's feet lifted high above his head and as Gunner began his airborne arc, so did Creeps. The hotdog, beer laden fan saw the determined eyes of a hungry canine flying toward his desired bounty just as the detail cop in the cruiser looked up to see the body of a middle aged, tall, dark haired Caucasian male break through the ball net behind the Green Monster. Creeps fell through the net landing sorely but unharmed on the hood of the cruiser all to the amusement of the radio listeners surrounding the car.

The cop was not amused. Surveying the dents in his hood and further irritated by the audacity of anyone who would cut into his game, he impatiently clamped the cuffs on Creeps and secured him to the car. He only took the time to say, "I'll read you your rights after the game," before returning to his radio.

On the other side the scene was completely congenial. By the time Gunner was in full flight, the fans had formed a human mattress around the beer and hotdog. Gunner's aim was right on the mark. As soon as he landed directly in front of the now laughing treasure-bearer, he gulped half the frank and was instantly lapping beer to wash it down. Naturally, this delighted the crowd who appreciated both the bravado and the appetite of their four-legged hero. They roared and applauded with pure enthusiasm.

Gunner knew he was being adored, but when he heard Nate's familiar whistle, he jumped the fence and ran across the field to rejoin his friend. An elated Nate knelt on the grass and spread his welcoming arms. In a manner uncharacteristic to any bulldog, Gunner leapt again, but this time only a few inches upward. Now feeling completely secure he put his feet on his friend's chest and licked his face. As the two headed toward the dugout, the crowd went wild.

So did Jack Davidson who witnessed the entire disaster on his screen. He picked up the bat beside his chair and swept his desktop clean.

~29~

Billy Ray's voice reflected the crowd's enthusiasm. "What a show. Looks like a happy reunion."

"And just in time for the game as the Louisburg Sluggers take the field to start the final inning of this slugfest," Clyde added.

Down below, Harmon had shaken off the stiffness caused by the delay and was warmed up and ready to go.

Once again donning his detective hat, Billy Ray leaned into the mic. "Slugfest is right, Clyde. We have a 25-24 game here today. That ties the top scoring game in the majors played back in 1922 when the Cubs beat the Phillies 26 to 23. There were fifty-one hits in that game and there have already been fifty-four today."

In the Slugger dugout, Nate and Jo worked to

regain their concentration following the hectic delay. "Have you seen Max?" Jo asked.

"They're checking him out at the first aid center."

"I hope he's okay?"

"He's beat up a bit, but he'll be all right," Nate said. He patted his daughter's hand and nodded toward the field to turn her attention back to the game. She looked up just as Curt Carter, the Sox right fielder, fouled a pitch.

"That's 0 and 2 on Carter" said Clyde. "Hudson appears as strong in the ninth as he was in the first."

As soon as the words left Clyde's lips, Harmon hurled a fastball past Carter for a call strike three. Carter was ushered back to the dugout by the wild cheers of every fan in the park as Mark Briscoe stepped into the box. The rhythm of the game had not been reestablished for either side, but Harmon was especially anxious to end his last appearance on the mound. He felt much different than before the delay. He took the signal and again burned the ball down the center of the plate with all he had in him.

Briscoe connected sending a line shot directly at Frizz Stephens head. The Slugger's shortstop had never seen a ball travel so fast. If he hadn't raised his glove to protect his face, the oscillating sphere would have hit him right between the eyes. For the crowd, what was merely a self-defensive move, turned into masterful glove work as Frizz executed the instantaneous catch.

The fans went crazy and so did Clyde Gooding. "Hudson blew that one down the center of the plate followed by a terrific catch by the shortstop Stephens. These Sluggers aren't letting up."

Even the victim Mark Briscoe had to smile as he walked back to the dugout past Johnny Daley on his way to the plate.

Daley took the first pitch low and outside, but had to go to the dirt on Harmon's second throw. The third pitch was even wilder going two feet above Cecil's reach. It was followed by a very slow wild pitch putting Daley on first.

"That was the first walk of the day for Hudson," commented Clyde. "He's showing signs of fatigue. Lugo is on his way to the mound, but there's no action in the bullpen."

"It hasn't been that way for the Sox," Billy Ray added. "Dryden is bringing in Mendez to finish out the inning and the game. He's gone through his entire pitching staff. Both teams may be in trouble if we go into extra innings."

Little did he know that extra innings would bring complete disaster for Nate Lugo who in no way wanted to hear what Harmon was about to tell him. He knew the news was bad when he saw the distress in Harmon's face. Nate casually lifted the ball from his young pitcher's glove and gently rubbed it between his hands. "Stay calm, Kid. You're about to close this game."

Harmon looked up into Nate's eyes. "It's over."

"What are you talking about?"

"It's worn off, Coach. The Cinderella effect. I was the last player programmed. None of us have it anymore." His young brow furrowed as he asked, "What do I do?"

Nate didn't like the look that should never be on any teenager's face, let alone one of his kids. Remaining composed, he rubbed the ball again as if warming a fertile egg for a hen to hatch, then gently laid it back into Harmon's glove. He smiled, put his hand on Harmon's shoulder and confidently said, "I know exactly what we're going to do." With that he leaned in closer to quietly relate his instructions.

Jack Davidson was watching the action when the smiling chief of security dropped the black bag on his desk. Davidson returned the smile as he ripped open the zipper. But the smile soon faded as he rifled through the gym clothes strewing them in his desperate search for the helmet.

Totally frustrated and completely irate, he

extended a handful of sweaty garments toward the guard. "What the hell is this?"

The chief of security stood frozen with a confused look on his face.

"Get out of here," Davidson yelled. "Go on. Get out."

The frightened guard sped out of the office leaving his boss in the middle of his newly made mess. Davidson picked up the empty bag, threw it on top of a sneaker lying near his desk, and turned his attention back to the game just in time to hear Clyde say, "This could be an injury."

The smile gradually returned to Davidson's face as he watched Nate Lugo place his hand on his ace pitcher's shoulder. He calmly sat down, picked up his Babe Ruth ball and turned his full attention back to the action. He let out an elated "Ha," followed by "Gotchya," as he tossed the ball from hand to hand.

Nate Lugo smiled at the crowd as he returned to the Slugger dugout. So did Roger Gray, but his interest was limited to the girls who giggled among themselves and adoringly waved back at the left fielder. Nate too eventually locked onto a certain lady holding a content Bichon Frise. He waved, but the fans, thinking the wave and smile were for them, responded in-kind letting out a cheer that brought even a broader smile to Nate Lugo's face.

As he stepped down into the dugout, Jo seemed desperate. "We have to win this, Dad."

Nate put his arm around his daughter's shoulder and continued to smile. "We've already won, Jo. Have some fun."

~30~

For the first time in the game, Harmon Hudson was alone on the mound. And after his talk with Coach Lugo, he actually didn't mind. He concentrated on the plate as Rick Collazo took his practice swings and stepped into the batter's box set for the 100 M.P.H. pitches he had faced all day. Harmon nodded to Cecil's signal before deliberately letting loose a high arcing slow pitch.

Colazzo clocked it.

"It's a high hard hit to the gap in deep left-center," exclaimed Clyde more excited than he'd been since the delay. "Both Grey and Chavez are running for it. They may be able to play it."

Roger Grey should have caught the ball, but he was slow, But not so slow as to block Clyde's view of the fleet of foot Harold Chavez who in a moment of brilliance made a low backhanded stab.

The disappointment in Clyde's voice emanated throughout the park and over the radio waves. "A misplay by Grey as he..."

But then he saw the beaming Chavez running toward the dugout. The center fielder lifted his left arm high towards heaven to reveal the ball in his glove. Clyde screamed into the mic, "Chavez has caught the ball. Chavez has caught the ball. What a catch. What a catch."

Not a seat in Fenway Park was occupied. The entire crowd was on its feet wildly cheering the smiling center fielder. The peppy Chavez still had his glove in the air when his fellow players swarmed him, hugged him, lifted him and slapped his back so much that it should have been hurting.

But the only thing Harold Chavez felt was the adoration of his teammates.

Jack Davidson watched it all, still nervously tossing the ball from hand to hand. "Lucky catch," he said to himself. "But luck won't be enough."

~31~

When the Sluggers had settled down, Jo Lugo understood immediate action had to be taken. "Time to recharge, and quick," she said following Harmon into the dugout. Her eagerness turned to confusion as soon as she looked in the corner. Sitting where the black bag should have been was a bruised and bandaged Max Roebuck. She turned to Nate. "Dad, the helmet's been stolen."

"It's not stolen," Max explained. "Professor Hudson has it."

Still confused, Jo's look shifted between Max her father. "We need it. What are we going to do?"

"We're gonna play ball," Nate said assuredly. "Not to worry." Knowingly he clapped his hands together and winked at Jo. "Who's up?"

"Me, Coach," answered Roger. "Then Luther and D.A."

"The three of you come over here."

Nate led them to the on-deck area. They drew in close and leaned forward in order to hear every word of his instructions. When he finished laying out his plan, Nate smiled as his eyes moved quickly from boy to boy. All three smiled back and nodded. To seal the deal Roger laid the end of his bat in the center of the circle and looked at the others. Luther and D.A. put their bats next to his, head to head.

Nate clapped his hands and threw his arm over Roger's shoulder. "Okay, Loverboy. Now's your chance. The girls are watching."

Roger Gray was not thinking about girls or anything other than the job at hand as he walked toward the plate in Fenway Park. His focus was so intense that he didn't even hear his own name as Clyde's voice rang over the speakers, "Leading off for the Sluggers is left fielder Roger Gray facing the new Sox pitcher Jose Mendez hoping to maintain a one run lead in the bottom of the ninth."

Roger could not believe the speed of the ball. It made Sonny Pep's pitches seem like they were thrown by a third grader. He took the first two, a fastball then a curve, both strikes. He grimaced but then stepped back into the box and faced Mendez with a look of utter determination. The third pitch, a Jose Mendez fastball, barreled right down the pike.

Roger concentrated and with all of his might swung directly at the white blur.

He was completely overpowered.

"Strike three," the umpire yelled motioning so dramatically even the furthest spectator in the top row of the bleachers could see the call.

Roger apologetically approached Nate standing at the edge of the dugout. "Sorry, Coach," he said, "but it was right down the middle."

"It's okay, kid," Nate said. "You did your best." Then he smiled and added, "At least you're swinging at the right pitches."

Nate turned his attention to Luther. "Did you hear him? Fast ball down the middle. This is your chance. Go get him."

Luther nodded and headed to the plate. He felt like every set of eyes in the park were on him. They were. Including the Sox bench and managers who were quietly riveted on the action. The fans had quieted down too, enough to evoke a comment from Billy Ray Block. "The crowd is awfully quiet here in the bottom of the ninth as we're down to the last two outs of the game."

Luther positioned himself as Mendez shook off a signal and then nodded. He watched the ball leave Mendez's hand. The pitch curved beautifully to catch the corner of the plate for a call strike.

"Perfect pitching for Mendez so far," said

Clyde. "Four pitches. Four strikes." Then he added from his ideal vantage point, "The windup. The pitch. A fastball."

In the thousands of times Luther Gordon had laid down a practice bunt, he had never executed one to the degree that he did at that moment. Clyde's enthusiasm once again peaked. "A perfect bunt down the first base line."

The ploy caught the Sox infield totally off guard. Playing him as they had in his previous eight trips to the plate, they were deep and straight away. By the time they adjusted, he had scurried down the first base line and crossed the bag before the ball.

The crowd wildly broke the silence. Even the detail cop in the cruiser was screaming under the silent Creeps now handcuffed to the roof.

—7 The noise at the Elizabeth Diner was deafening. Boss, lifted from his seat beside the radio, stood facing the full house and thrust both fists in the air. "That's our boy," he yelled. "That's our boy."

—7 Once more the seats at Fenway were empty. The standing, cheering crowd had no idea what to expect next. The Sox lined the fence of their dugout still quiet and focused, but the Louisburg Sluggers, as excited as the crowd, were on their feet clapping and showering gestures of elation.

"It couldn't be better," said Billy Ray. "That one sure surprised everyone."

Back in his office, Jack Davidson thought it could be much, much better. He nervously tossed the ball from one hand to the other as his eyes remained bolted to the screen.

~32~

If for nothing else than to settle his pitcher after an unexpected bump, Elliot Dryden signaled time and started to the mound to confer with Mendez.

"Dryden's on his way to the mound to talk with Mendez. That surprise move put the tying run on first and with the Slugger's cleanup hitter at bat, there's a lot to talk about," Clyde commented.

"It's been quite a day," Billy Ray said. "And it all comes down to two outs."

Knowing such delays can throw off a neophyte player, Nate Lugo watched carefully as D.A. took his practice swings He whistled to D.A., motioned and met him halfway down the third base line. Staring him directly in the eye and with a tone as much fatherly as coach-like, Nate encouraged him. "Son, it's right in you. You got it. I've seen it before, and I know what you can do." He placed his

neophy

179

hand on the young man's shoulder and slowly emphasized his next point, "But listen to the old man. You gotta spread your stance."

Nate continued his stare nearly mesmerizing D.A. until the young athlete nodded his understanding. Nate slapped his shoulder and walked back to take his place near third. D.A. approached the plate and with his new found confidence removed his cap and waved to the crowd. Doing so he revealed a carefully groomed fifties hairstyle known as a duck's ass or d.a.

Billy Ray laughed into the mic. "Puts an entirely different slant on his nickname. Would you look at that hairdo."

An equally amused Clyde reflected, "That takes us back a few years, doesn't it? The crowd certainly seems to appreciate it."

But his retro hairstyle wasn't the only new experience for the Fenway fans. For the first time, they watched D.A.'s pre-batting ritual. He hit the cleats of his right shoe with the end of the bat, then his left shoe. Once that was done, he immediately touched the bill of his cap with his right hand, slapped the St. Jude medal around his neck, dropped it further to pull his belt buckle before sliding the hand to the tip of the bat. Only then did he assume his stance.

The young batter's concentration was totally

focused on the ball delivered by the best closer in the league. The fastball steamed on the outside of the plate and past D.A.'s swing.

Nate whistled.

Once again D.A. looked to his mentor. Nate gestured for him to spread his stance. D.A. backed out, repeated the ritual and stepped back in the box, only this time with his feet a bit further apart. As the hurler's hand reached its apogee, D.A. detected a slight difference in the release and was able to get a piece of the curve ball sending it to the right of first base.

"Foul for strike two on this young slugger," commented Clyde.

Billy Ray nudged Clyde and smiled at the completed roster with the Sluggers lineup and their counterparts. Clyde looked at the list and gave Billy Ray the thumbs up for his brilliant detective work, sharp eye and equally astute memory.

Jack Davidson was still glued to the screen and still tossing the ball from hand to hand even harder and faster knowing he was a mere one strike away from the solution to his Fenway problem.

But the strike had to get past D.A. Nate once again signaled him to spread his stance. Following his repeated ritual, the now enlightened young man listened to the old man and spread his feet even wider. As soon as he set himself, he found that his center of gravity was perfectly distributed, a perfection so obvious to him that he glanced straight ahead and smiled at Nate who smiled back. D.A.'s focus blocked all sounds except for Jo's ever familiar chant of *Whatta ya say, D.A.* And then the intensity set in. Nature conspired with him to shut out all but his singular intention.

"It's 0 and 2," said Clyde, "Mendez nods. The stretch. The pitch. A fastball down the..."

The reaction of the crowd to the loud crack of the bat was as fast as Mendez's pitch. The temperature in the announcer's booth must have risen fifteen degrees in that split second as both Clyde and Billy Ray watched the shot rise toward the center of the Green Monster. "He's tagged it," Clyde screamed. But his intensity kept rising. "My god, what a shot. It's long. It's going. It's going. It's..."

D.A. didn't' hear anything except the bat hitting the ball and the sound of his own heart as he started down the first base line still watching the ball rise.

All Jack Davidson was able to see was a small white dot going out of the sight of the strategically placed cameras in his ballpark. The cadence and velocity of the ball he tossed from palm to palm was ever increasing as he chanted to the rhythm, "Another spoof goof. Another spoof goof."

Then he cracked. Losing all control, he stood and threw the ball attempting to apply the velocity of his ace pitcher. It was much, much slower than Mendez, but not too slow to shatter the huge screen into thousands of shards completely wiping out communication and creating complete silence.

Davidson leaned on his desk and motionlessly stared into space. The only movement in the office was the Babe Ruth ball slowly rolling across the plush green carpet. It came to a complete stop, hiding the trademark and autograph from Jack Davidson's view. When he shifted his focus, the only thing he saw were the red stitches on a plain, off-white baseball.

~ Postgame ~

Pretty good story, huh? But that's not all. Like I said at the beginning, that Independence Day had a profound effect on a number of lives.

Luther Gordon, Facie Fuller and Harold Chavez became neighbors in the Bellingham Development and continued their ongoing friendships, much closer than before.

Jack Davidson's real estate empire and bank account continued to grow as a result of the Bellingham Development and two others much like it. Following the game, he began negotiations to sell his team. The sale was finalized that November. Unlike Davidson, the new owners loved and understood baseball and the importance of the history of Fenway Park.

And they had to find a new head scout. Max Roebuck had relinquished that position to become a batting coach for the Red Sox. He also took quite a pay cut, but he felt mighty good about himself every time he plied the trade for which he had been so well groomed. Whenever the team was in town, he dined with Jo Lugo and both were more than happy to be graced with the other's company.

Richie D'Angelo, taking the advice of *the old man*, delayed his entry into the major leagues and accepted a scholarship to attend and play ball at Arizona State. After all, he had already proven his ability to play with the best of them. When talking with the recruiters, he insisted upon and received an important condition, admission and a scholarship for his future agent.

From that day on, neither Roger, Cecil nor Harmon had any problems getting dates. More often than not the girls came to them. All three became accustomed to hearing the question, "Isn't he cool?" They kept their hands in baseball as well occasionally appearing as guests on *Old Diamonds and New Fields*, which had quickly developed into the most listened to sports show on Boston radio.

Clyde Gooding and Billy Ray Block were more than pleased to once again fill the airwaves with their comments and decades of knowledge that they enthusiastically shared with the regional listeners. *Old Diamonds and New Fields* became so popular that it was picked up for national syndication in less than a year following its premier.

Their old friend never missed one of the shows since his work schedule had become so drastically abbreviated. This time he retired for good going out the way he wanted. As a winner. Sometimes, especially when his second wife was away at one of her legal conferences, he agreed to work late helping Freddy, who now solely owned the front room of Yesterday's News. (haw whwg)

On such nights after his former partner had left, Nate Lugo would sit quiet and content in the Inner Sanctum. He often looked at the newest addition to the room, a photo affectionately hung above the deed. Placing it on the table beneath the light, with only the sound of Gunner lapping beer, he would slowly scan the faces of the coaches, the mascot and the motley squad each proudly standing his ground in front of the Green Monster. During those moments, he felt like the richest man who had ever lived. He saw an old man reborn, surrounded by those who loved him. He had it all. Knowing they had played *The Game* the way it should be played always brought a smile to his face reflecting the larger smile in his heart.

neighborhood Boys —

Creps
Dark-haired
Caucasin

Rogu —
cevel
Hann.

CPSIA information can be obtained at www.ICGtesting.com
Printed in the USA
BVOW052037231011

274296BV00001B/4/P